Maurice Waller lives in S the south coast of England. *Home from Home* is his first novel for adults.

The Night Secret, published in 2015, was his first novel for children. He has written several short stories for children.

He has published two poetry anthologies, one for children and one for adults.

www.mauricewaller.co.uk

HOME FROM HOME

MAURICE WALLER

First published in 2017

Copyright © Maurice Waller 2017

ISBN 978-1-326-90972-7

www.mauricewaller.co.uk

Foreword

In these times of extensive migration, the issues of nationalism and identity have been brought into sharper focus than ever before.

This book begins in the South Africa of the apartheid era, when people were denied national identity because of their skin colour. The Nationalist government attempted to justify their policies by creating separate territories, called Bantustans, which were supposed to provide the various black peoples with homelands based on their ethnicity. It exposes the cruel irony of whites being allowed to come and go at will, while the movements of black people are constrained regardless of where they were born.

The final section is set in contemporary Israel and develops the theme of national identity and its associated paradoxes. It casts a spotlight on the policy of the Law of Return which allows Jews from anywhere in the world to become citizens of that country by virtue of their birth right as Jews. This section confronts the repercussions of the birth of the Jewish state in 1948 for the daily lives of Palestinians, a people without a state.

This story of three generations of the Levy family, spanning four decades, provides the vehicle for an examination of the paradoxes and anomalies which make national identity such a complex issue in modern times.

Maurice Waller

FOR LAUREN

Home from Home

Dulce et decorum est in patria habitare

(It is sweet and fitting to live in one's country)

1977

Joseph stood outside the shack, the glow from his cigarette intensified by the darkness. Inside Miriam was asleep. The bed was too narrow for two people to sleep comfortably and he had lain awake for some time before deciding to go outside for a smoke. All was still and quiet.

It could have been the luminous eyes of a wild animal perforating the dark. However, as the 'eyes' grew larger it soon became evident that a vehicle was approaching. Joseph threw his cigarette to the ground and hurried inside. The black gradually grew to a warm yellow and two distinct beams swayed unsteadily, accompanied by the crunching of tyres on the dirt track. The vehicle slowed and stopped. The interior light came on, revealing two occupants as the doors swung open. They climbed out, switching on torches and slammed the doors shut. Their footsteps, muffled by the sand, were followed by loud banging on a door.

"Maak oop! Open up! Police!"

After a few moments, the door slowly opened. An anxious face flickered in the candlelight giving it a spectral quality.

"Excuse me master?"

"Joseph Mpahle. Joseph Mpahle. Waar is hy?"

"No master. No Joseph here."

"Where is he?"

"Not here master. No Joseph master."

One of the policemen barged into the house sending the candle flying from Miriam's hand. A torch beam scanned the room and stopped on a huddled figure sitting in the far corner, head buried under its arms. The other policeman moved towards him and pulled him to his feet as if he were a root vegetable. The young man did not struggle but raised his hands to protect his face.

"Come! Come with us!"

"Why? Why what I done?"

"You Joseph Mpahle? Show us your pass! Come on where is it? Show us!"

"No dompas master."

The policemen took an arm each and dragged him to the door. "Suka wena!" yelped Joseph, struggling to break free.

"Hamba! Los hom!" shouted another voice from the darkness.

And then they were gone, dragging Joseph to the police van. They threw him into the back of the van. It started up with a growl and disappeared into the dark.

***

Janice Levy looked down through the large gaps in the clouds at the barren landscape below. The Transvaal in winter was brown and bleak. She had forgotten how vast a country this was. Every now and then signs of human habitation appeared below: a farm or a small cluster of rural dwellings. Occasional signs of water. A dam.

A confusing frisson of anticipation disturbed her. Was she coming home? Where was home these days? She had spent the past three years of her life living in Israel. After graduating from Wits University, she had taken the opportunity to spend some time on a kibbutz. Following five months of kibbutz life she had taken an office job in Tel Aviv, working as a secretary for a South African-born accountant, who had emigrated with his family in 1970.

Life in Tel Aviv had infiltrated her core and she felt settled now in her shared two-bedroom apartment. She had begun to accumulate a large circle of friends. Fluent in Hebrew, she had assimilated into Israeli life to such an extent that, on first meeting, there was little to distinguish her from any other young Israeli woman.

The plane was about thirty minutes from landing in Johannesburg. She had not been on South African soil for three years and she wondered what her reaction would be on seeing her homeland again. Moreover, how would she react to her family and friends? To what extent had they changed, if at all, in the years she had been away? How would she respond to their prejudices? Would their political views have stagnated, as she had suspected, judging by the correspondence of the last three years? She herself had changed, but how much? Would the gulf have widened between her and those with whom there were otherwise close bonds?

Janice fastened her seatbelt and tucked her magazine neatly into the pouch at the rear of the seat in front. The outskirts of urban Transvaal were now evident below and the cloud cover had thinned considerably.

***

Jan Smuts airport thronged with people awaiting the arrival of flight SA321 from Tel Aviv, amongst others. Strategically positioned at the front were Martin and Rina Levy. Martin scanned the passengers as they came into view from behind the screen that separated them from the outside world. A look of expectancy on each face was replaced by sudden recognition as someone familiar came into focus amongst the waiting crowd.

"She's had her hair cut short!" blurted Rina suddenly.

Janice emerged from behind a group of passengers. Grinning broadly, she abandoned her trolley and rushed forward to greet her parents. While Rina and her daughter were locked in an embrace, Martin retrieved the errant, driverless trolley. After a minute or so of muffled exclamations of delight Janice released her mother and flung her arms around her father's neck. Martin was overcome with emotion, unable to talk. Tears flowed freely down his cheeks as he clung to her as if terrified she would suddenly leave again.

***

The Levys made their way to the car park, Martin pushing the laden trolley awkwardly across the tarmac outside the airport building. The Mercedes boot more than coped with Janice's luggage and the various small bags containing gifts and other purchases from Tel Aviv's duty free shop.

Having threaded its way out of the car park, soon it was speeding along the freeway towards Johannesburg's Houghton suburb. Inside the vehicle Janice and Rina were engaged in an animated conversation about the former's latest boyfriend back in Israel. He was a Jerusalem doctor whom Janice had met six months ago.

"What's his name?" asked Rina.

"Yossi. Yossi Barlev. Before you ask, yes it is serious and yes he has asked me to move in with him. But ..."

"Move in with him? Are you sure that's the right-"

"I was just about to say mother – I can't do anything at the moment as I've been called up to the army," said Janice, gently chastising her mother's presumption.

"The army! My God! My daughter in the army! What next?!"

"It's what daughters who live in Israel do. It's a fact of Israeli life."

"Both my children in the army!" Rina was incredulous. Their son Jonathan was already doing his basic nine months' training in the South African army.

Martin remained silent, concentrating on negotiating the busy, at times frenetic, roads of Johannesburg. However, the faint smile that had appeared on his face at the start of the discussion about Janice's love life had soon disappeared on hearing his daughter was to become a soldier in the Israeli army.

"How is Jonnie? When will I see him?" asked Janice, attempting to steer the conversation along a different path.

"He's coming home this weekend. He's managed to get another pass. I don't know how he does it. He's been home twice already in the past two months. No doubt his young *shiksa* has something to do with it," tut-tutted Rina.

"Mom! I wish you wouldn't talk like that. So what if he hasn't got a nice Jewish girl-friend."

Rina remained silent. She didn't take kindly to being told off by her daughter. She found it difficult to accept that her son had not seen fit to choose from the hundreds of young Jewish women in Johannesburg. She had taken personally his apparently deliberate provocation in choosing to go outside the accepted circle. His girlfriend was "a nice enough young lady" but not really "one of us" and certainly not good enough for her son.

The remaining ten minutes of the drive back home was filled with a long, somewhat awkward and inappropriate silence. The Mercedes sped along the freeway linking the airport to the city of Johannesburg. Janice was momentarily surprised by the vastness of the landscape and the redness of the soil. The industrialisation of the link road soon usurped the scenery as factories and large advertising displays glided past on either side. In the distance the Post Office Tower thrust itself skywards rising against a backdrop of skyscrapers. Jo'burg, as she was known to all, was developing into a city with a distinctly Americanised vibrancy and pace.

Soon the exclusive white suburbs of Johannesburg provided a different context to her homecoming. Small, neat bungalows began to give way to larger homes set in expansive properties. The Mercedes eventually slowed and turned into a long driveway, lined either side with lavender trees. Autumn was already leaving its mark and leaves were an attractive rusty red. The car stopped in front of the double garage adjoining the house. A large boxer and an even larger ridgeback appeared at the side of the vehicle, their deep-throated barking welcoming its familiar occupants. Janice opened the door and greeted them enthusiastically. The ridgeback had been a three-month-old puppy the last time she had seen it, while the boxer was showing his eleven years as he dragged his rear legs along. The front door of the double-story house opened and a black woman and man came striding out to greet them.

"Hello Mary! How are you my friend? It's been a long time!" Janice embraced the woman enthusiastically. "Hello Jacob."

"Hawu nkosazana look beautiful!" Mary stood back as if admiring a work of art.

Martin opened the boot of the car and Jacob responded spontaneously, removing the large suitcase and taking it up to Janice's bedroom.

Janice took time to take in the garden and feel the relative warmth of the Johannesburg autumn sunshine before entering the house. The familiarity of it all embraced her and resonated, stirring a wealth of emotions from the past. Yet there was a foreignness about aspects of the house that every now and then surprised her. Paintings had been acquired, as had items of furniture. Her own bedroom had been used by several visitors in her absence; a new set of curtains framed the view into the rear garden and the addition of a desk and a rug hinted that a subtle shift in her status in the Levy home had evolved during her absence.

Although she had stepped back into a familiar world, she was filled with confused thoughts and feelings. She felt disorientated and detached – a foreigner in her own country.

Jacob returned to help Martin with the remaining bits and pieces that Janice had brought with her. When they had deposited them in Janice's bedroom, Joseph lingered, obviously wanting to say something.

"Can I help you Jacob?"

"Please master. I want speak with master."

"Yes sure Jacob. I'll see you in the study after dinner. Can it wait?"

Jacob hesitated and then nodded reluctantly. He left the room and went back downstairs. Martin met his daughter on the landing. They embraced.

"Welcome home, darling. It's wonderful to see you. You must be exhausted."

"Wonderful to be home. I am a bit tired. Maybe something to drink first and then I think I'll lie down for a while."

Martin smiled and cupped her cheeks gently in his large hands. "Of course. You must be exhausted. Let's have tea by the pool and then you can have a nap. See you downstairs."

**

"This is wonderful," sighed Janice. She lay on the lounger allowing the sunshine to gently warm her cheeks. "I could easily fall asleep right here."

"At least have your tea first," said Rina as Jacob wheeled the tea trolley onto the pool patio. "Thanks Jacob. Could you bring some sugar as well? Miss Janice likes sugar in her tea."

Martin came out to join them. "Isn't this amazing! All we need now is for your brother to arrive and the family unit will be back together again."

"When do you expect him?" asked Janice.

"He said he should be here by tomorrow night. A lot depends on *how* he gets here. Sometimes he takes the coach but he also thumbs a lift from time to time," said Martin.

"Is it easy for him to phone from camp?" asked Janice.

"Not really. There are two call boxes and they're mostly out of order. When he spoke to us last week he said he was aiming to leave on Friday morning."

Rina poured the tea and Jacob returned with the sugar. "Thanks Jacob. Don't forget to lay three places for dinner tonight. Mary is cooking Miss Janice's favourite dish, baked salmon; so we need fish cutlery as well."

"Yes madam. Three places."

"Salmon! I haven't had salmon since I left. Fantastic!"

"So Jan, how does it feel to be home?" asked Rina, passing her daughter a cup of tea.

"It's all very weird. It's home but in some respects it's not. Israel feels like home now."

"Three years isn't all that long though."

"No it isn't but you're talking to someone who hasn't ever really felt settled here. I always wanted to travel and if it hadn't been Israel then it might have been somewhere else."

"You look so relaxed lying there," said Rina. "Maybe you shouldn't bother going upstairs for a sleep."

"No I think I will. I also need to unpack and hang up some of my clothes." Janice stood up and kissed her parents before going up to her bedroom.

Having closed the bedroom door, she stood in the middle of the room for a few moments taking it all in. She had grown up in this room. From being a little girl of seven when they first moved in to their house in Houghton, experiencing the pubertal transition to teendom and eventually leaving for Israel as a graduate, this little room had been her personal fiefdom. Here she had spent private and intimate moments. She had slept, studied and entertained friends of both sexes. On the bed nestled between two cushions was her twenty-three-year-old ragdoll. The colours had faded and the stitching on one of the seams needed attention. A remnant of her formative years in this room. Much else had changed. New curtains fell onto an unfamiliar wall-to-wall carpet, replacing her rug which had been moved to the conservatory. Her desk had been replaced with a larger oak version with an accompanying swivel chair. It dawned on her that she had left home. Physically and emotionally. She felt like a visitor.

***

Later that night, after dinner, Jacob met Martin in his study. Martin sat at his oak desk, his body weight stretching the leather chair's mechanism to its limit as he leant back, hands behind his head. Jacob stood subserviently in the middle of the room, his eyes fixed on the carpet.

"What's it, Jacob? Is there a problem?"

Jacob did not look up. He didn't like to make eye contact with his boss. He spoke hesitantly.

"My son, Joseph............ he in police jail."

"In jail? Do you know why?"

"No *dompas*."

"No pass? Why's that?"

Jacob remained silent. Martin tried his best to hide the irritation he was beginning to feel.

"Where was he arrested?"

"Jo'burg ... Soweto."

"What here in Jo'burg! I thought he was in the Transkei."

"Joseph, he come to Jo'burg from Transkei master."

"When did they arrest him?"

Joseph hesitated, sensing the irritation behind the question.

"Last night master," he mumbled eventually.

"How long has he been in Jo'burg?"

"Two month master."

Martin leaned forward causing the chair to squeak loudly. It was a harsh sound which seemed to aggravate the situation and Jacob moved back slightly, feeling even more uncomfortable. "Oh dear ....shit man.............. He's a bloody fool you know. He can't just come here from the Transkei without permission." Jacob remained silent, his eyes fixed on the carpet. "I'm not sure there's anything I can do Jacob," continued Martin. "I'll find out more tomorrow. I can also speak to boss Harry Silver .... I don't know, Jacob .... as far as I can see he'll have to go back to the Transkei."

Martin looked expectantly at the greying man before him. Jacob's patchy beard was interspersed with wisps of silver. His fifty-eight-year life story was etched on his prematurely furrowed brow. The 'whites' of his dark eyes were yellowed and reddened from years of drinking homemade beer and frequenting smoke-filled *shebeens*. Jacob remained silent, briefly glancing up at Martin and returning his stare to the carpet below.

"Jacob....I'll see what I can do. You'll have to give me all the details before I leave for the office in the morning." There was a brief period of silence and hesitation. Then Martin leaned forward emphatically. "Right Jacob, I'll see what I can do."

Jacob took that as his cue to leave. "Thank you master."

***

That night in his *khaya*, Jacob snuffed out the candle and got into bed. He lay on his back for a long time before finally drifting into a fitful sleep. His dreams that night were a montage of images from the past. His family back home in the Transkei; his late wife Thembeka, their three children, Joseph the eldest, now a young man aged twenty-two, Goodness, the only girl, nineteen and Gideon, the youngest, a boy of sixteen; his home, a hut in a remote village, some thirty kilometres from the capital, Umtata.

He woke up to relieve himself. He shone his torch on the clock ticking loudly beside his bed. It was almost three o' clock. He groped his way towards the cubicle adjoining the room and urinated into the hole in the concrete floor. On his return the torchlight fell upon the black and white image of his son beside the clock. It had been taken when Joseph was twelve. A twelve-year-old who played in the bush with his friends. In those days Jacob worked on the mines in Johannesburg. He had missed the best years of his children's lives. He managed to go home once every two years at Christmas to spend a fortnight with the family. It was during those brief spells that Jacob had forged a strong bond with Joseph.

Jacob lay awake a while, reminiscing and regretting. He felt helpless – more useless as a father than ever. His son was lying in a police cell somewhere else in Johannesburg and he was unable to do anything about it.

Eventually Jacob fell asleep again. He dreamt of his time as a young man working in the gold mines of Johannesburg. Crammed into a cage with the stench of sweaty bodies; the clanking of the seemingly endless, darkening descent. His body was swirling and spinning – cocooned in an ever darker, ever faster vortex. And then he was floating gently like a feather. Devoid of control.

The loud ringing in his ears told him it was 5.30 a.m. and time to get up and face the day. He lay in bed listening to the sounds from the room next door. Mary was up and about, getting herself ready.

Jacob yearned for Thembeka. She had died after contracting tuberculosis when she moved back to the Transkei. The children had been looked after by her parents who both died soon after. Jacob's sister had taken them, and had done a good job bringing them up.

He missed Thembeka's body against his at night. He missed the smell of lovemaking. The loneliness of the khaya at night had taken its toll over the years. His relationship with Mary had almost broken down and he was still in the process of repairing the damage caused by a night of recklessness following a visit to a shebeen in Alexandra. He had been out drinking with some friends and, having walked the three miles from the nearest bus stop, he had been feeling particularly low, a mixture of the influence of very potent beer and a prolonged spell of homesickness. On arriving back at the Levys' house he stumbled outside Mary's room banging his head on a lead downpipe outside. Unfortunately, his forehead caught a bracket causing a gash. When Mary came out to investigate she was alarmed to see blood pouring from his head and immediately helped him to his room where she tended his wound with cotton wool and water.

Eventually Mary stemmed the flow of blood and the two of them found themselves in a somewhat compromising position with Jacob's head in her lap and her hand cupped over his ear. In his drunken state Jacob misread the situation and began to exploit the perceived serendipity of the circumstances. Placing a hand on her breast he began to explore her thigh with the other. Mary reacted by standing up and shouting at him as he fell to the floor. Undeterred, Jacob got back onto his feet and forced himself on her, provoking a high-pitched scream which in turn caused the dogs to begin barking. Mary slammed her hand across Jacob's face. "Suka wena! Suka!" she shouted as Jacob grabbed her arms and pinned her to the wall forcing his beer-drenched mouth onto hers.

Jacob lay in bed for a while trying to recall the events of that night. Nothing was clear. He had learnt afterwards that Martin Levy had entered with both dogs and had dragged him away from Mary, pushing him onto the bed where he had lain all night until waking the next morning with the worst headache he had ever known. He had received a final warning from Martin who not only threatened him with dismissal but also promised to call in the police should it ever happen again.

The relationship between Jacob and Mary had been strained ever since but time seemed to be healing the wounds, albeit slowly. The subject had never come up again although both were usually aware of the other's thoughts when left alone together in the house.

It was still dark outside and none of the morning sounds had been switched on. Jacob got up, lit a candle and began his ablutions. There was something robotic about his movement as he prepared for his day's work. He donned his 'boy's' overall. He spread the blanket over the coir mattress and tucked it under. He took five minutes or so to gather himself while he sat on the edge of his bed.

There was a knock on the door. The candlelight revealed two shoes in the gap at the bottom of the paneled wooden door.

"Ngena!" grunted Jacob, and Mary entered with a bowl of steaming porridge and a mug of tea. Jacob thanked her and warmed his hands on the enamel tea mug. He took a few minutes to have his breakfast before snuffing out the candle.

It was still dark outside as he left the *khaya*, closing the door behind him. The kitchen lights were on in the Levy house but the rest of the rooms were still in darkness.

***

"Word wakker! Kom Kom! Get up you lazy little shits!"

Jonathan Levy's dream was broken. The voice of Corporal Du Toit had exploded his sleep and the offensive reality of the military camp was suddenly with him. He sat up and the brightly-lit room of his barracks offended his eyes. The bedclothes on the bunks on either side of his were stirring. It was dark outside. A glance at his watch revealed it was 2.00 a.m. The corporal was walking up and down the middle aisle, which separated two rows of bunks, barking his Afrikaans orders metronomically.

The instructions were to remove their pyjamas and line up outside, naked. They had two minutes to be on parade.

It was a starlit night and an ice-cold breeze ruffled his pubic hair as he stood to attention on the dusty ground. He resisted the temptation to move his arms from his side or to move one foot to another. The consequences of revealing any discomfort were simply not to be contemplated. The corporal was like a lioness scanning a herd for the most vulnerable and at the first sign of weakness he would pounce and savage the victim mercilessly.

Since joining the camp near Kimberley two months before, this had been a weekly occurrence. Usually the pretext was that someone in the barracks had committed a 'major' offence. Examples of these 'major offences' were failure to ensure that shoes were kept neatly under the bunk or that a rifle was visible to any visitor entering the room. Such attempts at ironic humour had long since ceased to rile Jonathan.

On the customary command the men ran naked, two by two, down to the swimming pool area about half a mile from the main camp. The corporal lined them up at the side of the pool. On the whistle the twenty young men dived in and swam to the other side. They climbed out and lined up again in their twos. They ran back to the camp, where they dried themselves and got back into bed.

In the bunk next to Jonathan's, Norman Sheldon was whimpering uncontrollably. Ever since arriving Norman had been unable to cope with the rigours of military life. Slowly but surely Norman was cracking up. The more he demonstrated his discomfort the more he was picked on by the corporal and staff sergeant in charge of his platoon. The extra 'spare tyre' around his waist made him even more of a target for such military bullying.

Eventually the whimpering died down and Norman fell into a fitful sleep.

Jonathan lay awake for some time. His mind was filled with thoughts of his girlfriend Helen whom he was due to see during the coming weekend trip back home. He thought about his sister who lived so many miles away and was now waiting to see him back in Johannesburg. He considered what they had in common. They shared the same parentage and had been brought up in the same household. Yet, that aside, there was very little that bound them. Jonathan resented her attachment to Israel and her regular criticism of the lives of those she had left behind. Her political 'shenanigans' had annoyed the entire family, including those members beyond the immediate Levy household. Martin's brother Abe had warned that Janice was likely to land herself in 'a spot of bother', if she continued to associate herself with young people who were on the government's radar.

Yes, Jonathan resented having to give up so much time to serve in the SA army. Yes, he would rather be doing something more constructive with his life right now. But he also knew that this was his home, his homeland. If he was called on to fight for his country, he would. And that fact made him determined to make the most of army life. He had long ago decided that he would knuckle down and see out his time with minimal resentment. That was his present lot in life and there was little he could do to change it. Moreover, as he had been told so many times by so many people, including his father, the army makes men out of boys. "It'll toughen you up," his Uncle Abe had said.

He looked across at the figure in the bed next to his. Norman was snoring now and seemingly at peace. But Jonathan knew it was only a matter of time before Norman cracked completely.

***

"Hello Harry, how's it going with you? .... No I'm fine thanks. ....Yes I'm still on for golf. I'm phoning for a different reason .... just a little problem my servant boy Jacob's got right now....Yes I need some advice. ..... it's about his son. He's been arrested for being in Jo'burg without a pass..... two nights ago ..... he's from the Transkei....... "

The telephone receiver was securely gripped between Martin's jaw and shoulder while he signed the pile of papers his secretary had placed before him. Harry Silver was an experienced attorney in Bantu Law and had seemed the obvious choice when it came to pursuing the case of Jacob's son Joseph. If anyone could advise it would be Harry. Quite fortuitously they were due to play golf that afternoon so Martin felt some preparatory briefing might help expedite matters.

Martin Levy replaced the receiver, cupped the back of his neck with both hands and leant back in his chair. His head just touched the wall behind and he blew a deep sigh. There was a knock at the door and a petite young woman entered, without waiting for a response. She was dressed in a smart navy blue top with matching skirt and her short hair was neatly trimmed, giving her a 'Julie Andrews' look. A pair of spectacles dangled from a chain around her neck. She walked over to Martin's desk and placed a bundle of papers before him.

"More signing?"

"I'm afraid so Mr. Levy. I have to get them in the post this afternoon. Aren't you meant to be leaving soon?"

"I'll just finish signing these Steph and I'll be on my way."

Martin was due to attend a luncheon organised by the South African Zionist Federation. The visiting speaker was a Professor Goldblum from Jerusalem University and the topic was "The Role of Zionism in the Diaspora." For much of his adult life Martin's relationship with the State of Israel had been mostly tangential. He had yet to make the pilgrimage to Israel, but now that his daughter was living there and had seemingly decided to settle there for the long haul, his commitment to the cause had grown stronger and a visit was a likelihood in the not too distant future, if not, imminent. He had reached the view that it was the duty of Jews in South Africa to give whatever support they could to the cause of the Jewish homeland. His acceptance had become unconditional, founded on years of inculcation as was customary for a high profile member of the local Jewish business community. From an early age as a boy growing up as a Jew it had been de rigeur to support the building of the Jewish state.

His commitment to his religion was rather half-hearted and his attendance at synagogue was confined to the High Holy Days, celebrations such as weddings and the occasional family barmitzvah. He could read Hebrew from the prayer book yet with very little understanding. Rina did not bother about keeping a kosher kitchen, although pig products were banned. His son Jonathan had celebrated his barmitzvah with all the usual trappings and associated festivities. Yet the so-called transition to religious adulthood had faded soon after and Jonathan had followed a largely secular course towards his late teens.

A short while later Martin left the building where he had spent the greater part of his adult working life, originally learning the business from his uncle Jack Levy and now as CEO of Goldblatt and Levy Wholesalers. Uncle Jack and Solomon Goldblatt had founded the business in the early 1950s and it had grown into a thriving concern, selling a range of office equipment to some of the largest businesses in the Transvaal. After Solly Goldblatt had passed away in

1966, Jack had run the business until his retirement, when he passed complete control over to Martin. It was Martin's wish that *he* in turn would one day pass the baton over to Jonathan. He was keen to secure the future of the business and despite Jonathan's intention to travel after his army training, he was sure that one day his son would take over.

Martin hated any interruption to the smooth tenor of his life and the business with Jacob's son had unsettled him. He resented having to take on the burden of responsibility, despite his understanding of the consequences of the government's apartheid policy. It was enough having to cope with the irritation of Jacob's various foibles and misdemeanours without having to deal with his son's problem. Unlike his daughter, he preferred to remain politically neutral as much as possible. At general elections he always voted for the official opposition United Party, which seemed the safest option. It was socially unacceptable in Johannesburg Jewish circles to vote for the governing Nationalists but unlike others in Houghton he could not bring himself to vote for the Progressives. He eschewed what he regarded as their dangerous policy of a 'qualified franchise', which would mean ultimate domination by the blacks. When pressed, he felt things were just about alright as they were with the various black 'nations' being encouraged to settle in independent Bantustan 'states'. Politics was something other people did and his only involvement was every four to five years when the political parties solicited his support.

As much as he loved his daughter deeply she had developed the art of getting under his skin when it came to politics. He always found it difficult to argue against her opinions which were discomfiting to say the least.

"I'm more than happy to go about my life wearing blinkers," he once remarked when Janice chided him for supporting a party which effectively stood for a slightly softer version of apartheid. "I try to mind my own business and get on with my life, doing what's best for my family."

Johannesburg's traffic was particularly problematic that morning and Martin arrived at the synagogue in Greenside just in time for the luncheon, where he joined the other hundred or so invited guests, effectively a "who's who" of the Jewish business community's elite.

***

".....In conclusion friends, clearly modern Israel is dependent on its citizens in the Diaspora for survival. It is a young, vibrant and modern state but without external support it will never survive. But, again, I want to stress that it is no good for the State of Israel if Jews in the rest of the world cannot see further than their bank balance. We need your sons and daughters *in the flesh*, even if your *own* generation is not committed to that degree of Zionism. Yes we do need your money, but money alone won't buy us the secure future we can get from thousands of dedicated youngsters. That is why the Law of Return is so important to Israel and Jews around the world. Israel needs young, vibrant, zealous and committed young men and women citizens in order to survive. That was the lesson of the Yom Kippur War. Money can't defend a nation. Yes money can buy the weaponry, but ultimately the nation relies on its people to see off the enemy. Thank you."

Martin joined in the applause. The approval of the audience was evident and Professor Goldblum sat down, a broad grin illuminating his face. He raised his hand to the audience in acknowledgement.

Martin stayed for lunch where he became engrossed in a discussion about national loyalty with Simon Kuper, an old school friend of his who had recently left to live in Israel and was on a fleeting visit to attend his mother's tombstone consecration. Simon was adamant that Jews in the Diaspora were "living a lie" and to an extent were being unfair to the host country. He had come to realise that it was not enough to send funds to the Jewish homeland and that dual nationality was not an option either. Sport was one area where there might be a conflict of interest. Who would Martin support in a sporting contest between Israel and South Africa? Martin told him how he briefly hesitated over that very question in a recent volleyball contest between South Africa and Israel. When it came to sport it was always going to be South Africa, the country of his daily living. Martin followed volleyball in the papers and attended matches in Johannesburg when he could. He was familiar with the players and therefore found it a relatively easy choice when it came to deciding whom to support. Despite the boycott, the Israeli volleyball team had slipped into the country almost unnoticed and had managed to play a series of five games without provoking any fuss in the media.

"Ah but what would you do if came to war?" Simon confronted him with this question just as dessert was being served.

"Fortunately that's a hypo-"

"Yes, yes I know it's hypothetical but you never know Martin. History has a way of springing surprises on us. Anyway let's say, hypothetically of course, that Israel saw fit to befriend one of South Africa's neighbours, like Angola for instance. What would you do then? Who would you support?"

"I can't see that ever happening. Angola is a communist target anyway. And Israel would never be an ally of communism."

"Well.. let's take the anti-apartheid stance of the Israeli government. The official position of the Knesset is that South Africa should be condemned for apartheid."

"I can't say I'm comfortable with that," said Martin, beginning to sound irritated.

"Well Martin, when all is said and done, I think it's about deciding how you prioritise the labels that you wear as a human being. Which comes first in your identity hierarchy? Jew or White South African? If Jew, then you have to commit yourself to Israel."

"But to uproot myself at my age is not an easy, never mind clever thing to do. I'm not young and unattached anymore. My Janice is building a life for herself in Israel-"

"*I've* done it Martin. *I've* started a new life. I've given up a legal practice, a large five bedroom house for a new beginning."

"Yes and I admire you for doing that. But... but I'm not sure I could ever contemplate that. I'm content to live out my life here."

Martin wiped his mouth with his serviette and stood up. "Nice to see you Simon. I've got to be on the golf course in half an hour. Love to Sarah."

"You take care Martin my old friend. Give Rina a big kiss from her long time admirer."

Martin laughed, shook Simon's hand and left the room.

As he drove to the Houghton Golf Club he was preoccupied with thoughts of his family. His daughter was now a fully-fledged Israeli who had clearly made a life for herself in the Holy Land. This had lent an added significance to the substantial donation he was about to make to the professor's appeal. His son was doing his national service in the South African army, more than a thousand miles away. The likelihood was that Jonathan would eventually be sent to South-West Africa to fight against SWAPO. How did he feel about that? The propagandised line was that the South African forces were defending their country from future terrorist incursions, even though the enemy was not directly theirs. Indeed they were flying in the face of UN resolutions and despite its de facto status as a South African province, SWA was, de jure, still a protectorate, subject to UN jurisdiction.

Did he really admire Simon Kuper? Would he ever contemplate the same move? Martin preferred not to face that particular choice. Yes, he felt uneasy about the duality of his status as a Jewish South African. He was aware of the contradictory nature of his position as a donor to a foreign country, made all the more difficult to defend by the poverty and injustice in the land of his birth; widespread and deep-rooted poverty that required the urgent attention of white South Africans such as himself. Of course such introspection demanded the confronting of the fundamental question at the heart of the Diaspora: "What is Jewishness? What makes a Jew?"

Martin could count on one hand the visits he had made to his local synagogue during the past twelve months. Yes, his mother's Jewishness had attributed to him the right to uproot himself and arrive at Israel's doorstep and claim citizenship of that country. So was it more his race than his religion that afforded him that birthright? What then of his friend Jack Donovan? Jack had converted to Judaism but because it was the Judaism of the Reform variety there was some doubt as to his right to become an Israeli citizen if he so desired. Jack saw the inside of a synagogue more times in one year than Martin had done in his lifetime. Moreover, the question then arose: if to be a Jew is to be a member of a race how can one convert to membership of a race?

Not for the first time these questions swirled around inside Martin's head as he drove through Johannesburg's leafy Houghton suburb. And as usual he eventually managed to tuck the issues into a corner of his subconscious as his thoughts turned to the afternoon's golf. Why in recent times had he failed to play to anywhere near his handicap and why was his new driver not a match for the old one he had so readily discarded? Questions such as those forced themselves to the forefront of his mind as he turned into the driveway of Houghton Golf Club.

***

The afternoon Johannesburg sunshine belied the late autumn chill that rode on the breeze as Martin and his golf partner and friend, Harry Silver, strode purposefully towards the 1st tee. Following at a respectful distance behind the two men were their caddies, both young black lads who bore their burdens stoically, albeit with the confident air of experts. On reaching the tee each placed his bag on the ground and gestured to the two men to choose their clubs.

Martin's caddy wore a pair of old takkies while his colleague was more than happy to go barefoot. Their clothes underlined the incongruity against the background of one of the country's most exclusive golf courses and, while any overseas visitor might have been taken aback at such a discordance, there was nevertheless an air of normality about the foursome which traversed the course that afternoon.

It wasn't long before Martin took the opportunity to broach the subject of Jacob and his son Joseph.

"It's tough on them you know Harry. Jacob tells me that before his son came to Jo'burg he hadn't seen him for four years."

"Who knows what the solution is? There just aren't enough jobs to go round. Unfortunately, there has to be a way of controlling their movement."

"Of course. But it's still tough. Let's see if I can do better with this drive."

His caddie handed him his driver and Martin bent down to place his ball on the tee. He took a step backwards and lined up his ball with the target flag on the green some three hundred metres in the distance.

Martin steadied himself and swung his driver backwards tracing an arc to a zenith somewhere behind his head. On its downward path the club face met the ball with a 'clud'. His anguished cry was followed by an expletive which in turn was followed by "Can you believe it! If I'm not slicing I'm hooking!"

Harry chuckled and placed a consolatory arm around his friend," You can only get better. See you on the green."

A short while later the two men met on the first green. They took their putters from the caddies and went to study their balls which formed an equilateral triangle, each side three metres or so, with the hole.

"I feel I ought to make an effort for poor old Jacob. He's been with us a long time now." said Martin.

"What sort of boy is his son?"

"I don't really know him. It seems from what Jacob says that he is an honest young man who just wants to make a life for himself where the opportunities are. Nothing unusual about that."

"For sure. The problem is there are thousands - hundreds of thousands, if not millions like him. There's a limit to what this city can take."

"Right let's see if this ball will behave itself." Martin swung his putter gently back and in a pendulum motion brought it forward to strike the ball. "Go on ... go ...in you go! What control!" He punched the air and handed his putter back to the caddie.

"I've got some work to do now," declared Harry practising a fresh air putt. "Here goes."

The ball was struck firmly towards the hole and it dropped in obligingly. Martin and Harry made their way along a path towards the next tee, their caddies in tow.

"It's contagious. I'm following your example. So tell me, how is Janice enjoying her stay?"

"I *think* she's happy to be home. She's still full of nonsense though. She told me she felt uneasy living in our house after being away for so long."

"Uneasy? Why? What does she mean by that?"

"She's referring to the servants of course. Wait till her brother arrives. She's bound to have a row with him about the way he speaks to them. Rina tells me Steven passed his exam."

"Yes we're very pleased, not to say surprised. He doesn't know the meaning of the word "study". I wish he could take a snooker exam; he'd do us proud if he could. If you ever need Steven in an emergency just phone Joe's Snooker Parlour or whatever it's called."

"Let's hope you never *do* need him in an emergency. No good if you don't even know the name of the place."

"It's what happens next that concerns me. So, he will qualify with a B.A. degree next year and then what? There's no sign of any interest in or commitment to his future. Of course it's mandatory to travel these days." Harry's caddie handed him the driver as they arrived at the next tee.

"Where does he want to go, Harry?"

"Everywhere at this stage. He wants to start in Europe, probably the UK and end up in the Far East.

"How's Jess?"

"Jess is doing well. She's already starting to think about university. She wants to go to Cape Town."

"Does she still want to do medicine?"

"All being well, yes. Right let's see if I can stay on the fairway, this time."

The second hole was flanked by a mixture of stinkwood and oak trees in their late autumn attire on either side of the fairway. The clear sky was beginning to develop a silvery, wintry shimmer.

"We'd better get a move on if we want to play eighteen before the sun sets," said Martin.

Later the two men were loading their golf bags in the car park.

"I'll see if there's anything I can do about Jacob's son, Martin," said Harry. "The main thing is to get him out of jail and put him on a train to the Transkei as soon as possible."

"I suppose that's the best we can hope for. Thanks Harry see you soon."

"Love to Rina."

***

Jonathan picked up his bag and ran to the car which had stopped about twenty yards ahead. The driver wound the window down and leaned across the passenger seat. "Waar gaan jy? Where are you going?" he asked.

"Jo'burg or somewhere near if that's okay?"

"I can take you to Randfontein."

"Perfect – thanks a lot." Jonathan opened the back door and threw his backpack on to the seat. Removing his beret he scrambled into the front seat keeping hold of his R4 rifle.

"Been waiting long?"

31

"Not too bad. Mind you, not much traffic either."

"Hennie Van Niekerk."

"Jonathan - Jonathan Levy – pleased to meet you and thanks."

The driver of the vehicle turned up his radio and a commercial about tyres invaded the vehicle. The car's tyres screeched in response as it resumed its journey.

The road was long and straight and on either side were miles of flat, arid land punctuated by the occasional farmstead. The terrain was sprinkled with tiny spots of green and ringed by distant mountains.

"Where are you based?" asked Hennie Van Niekerk, raising his voice above the song on the radio.

"Just outside Upington."

"You've come a long way today."

"Ja lucky. Three lifts so far."

"You guys are doing a great job hey." Hennie Van Niekerk was middle aged, probably in his early fifties. He was thick-set with a neatly trimmed moustache which adorned a ruddy complexion achieved by a combination of sunshine and beer.

"I haven't had any action yet. They say we'll be sent to Caprivi next month."

"Caprivi eh – my mate's son was killed in Caprivi."

Jonathan didn't respond. He wasn't sure he wanted to know that. Very few people in his regiment seemed to understand the politics of the South West Africa situation or the status of the territory. It felt as though they were fighting somebody else's war. Jonathan had never been to SWA but those with first-hand knowledge had indicated that although it was almost regarded as a province of the Republic, the German influence gave it a distinct and somewhat different feel.

"Do you smoke?"

"Oh .. yes thanks." Jonathan took the proffered cigarette. Van Niekerk pushed the car's cigarette lighter firmly into the socket and it popped out a few seconds later. Jonathan had taken up smoking within a week of his arrival at the army camp. It seemed the obvious thing to do. At first he had hated it but he preferred to go with the group dynamic as far as smoking was concerned. Smoke breaks punctuated a typical army day and those who abstained were often confined to the periphery of the social gatherings that formed whenever a smoke break was declared.

Jonathan had soon learnt to enjoy smoking and it wasn't long before he was smoking twenty or so a day. He always felt calm and relaxed when holding a cigarette and now in the car with a stranger, smoking would probably help to form a bond between the two men for the rest of the journey. At least there was one thing they would have in common.

The radio was allowed a dominant role for the next fifteen minutes or so as the two men sat in silence. The road was long and straight. It stretched as far as the eye could see. On his side, in the distance he could just make out a line of mountains. The endless barrenness of the approaching winter on both sides of a largely empty, straight road made Jonathan feel strangely vulnerable. He put his head back and closed his eyes as a slow Bee Gees song wafted within the car.

"Ever killed anyone?" The question itself was like a gunshot. It took Jonathan by surprise and instinctively he tightened his hold on the rifle whose butt had been firmly gripped by the heels of his boots.

"No- no I- I haven't had to ... yet", he stammered, betraying the uncertainty the question had aroused within him.

"I have!"

"Oh..." Jonathan was somewhat taken aback. The declaration was flavoured with more than a hint of pride.

"Two kaffirs. My dogs were barking in the middle of the night and I went to investigate. I saw someone on the roof of the khaya. I shouted at him to get down. He ignored me so I fired a shot – I was trying to frighten him. It was too dark and I hit him - he fell off the roof. Unfortunately for him the dogs got there first ..... he never recovered."

"Shit."

"Ag man it was his own fault. "

"You said you killed two -"

"Ja. The other one was causing trouble at work. He was drunk and one of the girls said he raped her. I told him the police were coming to get him and he went for me. So I shot him."

Jonathan looked at his rifle. He felt sick. It was the matter of fact tone of voice that got to him. Jonathan had never thought about the prospect of actually firing his rifle at a living target. He had spent hours on the range firing at concentric circles and had never once extrapolated the prospect that one day it might be a person. He had winced at the use of the word 'kaffirs'. He had been the object of anti-Semitic abuse both at school and in the army and was fastidious about eschewing any form of racist language himself.

"You guys must be thirsting for action hey. When you go to Caprivi man, that's when it'll all happen. With that thing you can kill ten MPLA bastards in a minute."

Jonathan had nothing he wanted to say in response. Hennie Van Niekerk was the first civilian he had met who had spoken of killing someone as if it was part and parcel of living. He had been in the army for four months now and although there had been moments when it had been almost unbearable, that had been offset to some extent by the camaraderie he had experienced. Until now the common enemy among the troops had been Sergeant-major Van Tonder and one or two corporals. However soon the enemy would become something different. It would have a black face, it would possibly speak a version of Portuguese and it would be fighting to gain control of its own country. It would be someone he had never met and probably of his own age.

Jonathan was confused about his own position regarding the task ahead. On the one hand, he was a patriot and vowed he would never follow his sister's course and emigrate. On the other hand, he was unclear about the politics of the situation he found himself in. Conscription was part of growing up as a young white man in South Africa. Your black 'compatriots' had their own homelands and were officially regarded as mere 'visitors' when living in 'white' South Africa. The option he had chosen was to bury his head in the sand when it came to politics and do what most other young South African males had opted to do.

"If you bury your head in the sand you get your arse kicked in," someone had once said. "The time will come when your skin colour will be a disadvantage. Now you should stand up and be counted. This can't go on forever you know." The advice had come from his sister's boyfriend at the time, a young man whose ANC allegiance had meant he was ensconced in a prison cell somewhere in the Pretoria area. So for the time being Jonathan's head remained firmly buried, mostly in the desert sands of the Kalahari.

Jonathan began to feel sleepy and struggled to stay fully awake. However, the drone of the vehicle and the constant radio music soon lured him into a doze. He made sure his rifle was secured between his thighs and the sling was wound round his wrist.

Gradually the rural surrounds of the past couple of hours merged into something more urban.

"If I drop you at the bus terminus you should be able to get to Jo'burg before it gets dark." Jonathan's light slumber was interrupted by his companion's gravelly voice.

"That'll be great thanks." Jonathan had begun to feel a little claustrophobic in Van Niekerk's pick-up truck and was looking forward to stretching his legs.

A short while later he was deposited at Randfontein's bus terminus. The young soldier weighed down by a large rucksack and rifle slung over his shoulder was surrounded by evening commuters thronging the pavement. His was the only white face. Within seconds a clear space about a metre and a half in diameter had formed spontaneously around him. A combination of his skin colour and the military uniform was clearly a power factor in terms of his public status and the crowded terminus responded accordingly. Then he noticed a row of three telephone kiosks across the road and, neatly negotiating his way through the slalom of rush hour traffic, he joined the shortest queue. When the woman inside had completed her call the two people in front dutifully stepped aside and waved Jonathan through. He hesitated, but they were insistent so he proceeded to make his call.

"Hello Ma, it's Jonathan. Can Dad fetch me please?"

***

Jonathan and Janice had grown up together but also separately. Their respective social milieux and political views had always diverged to the extent that from time to time heated discourse was part and parcel of dinnertime in the Levy household.

Janice's strong liberal, anti-Nationalist and radical views contrasted starkly with Jonathan's somewhat apolitical acceptance of the status quo. Nevertheless, when brother and sister were reunited an hour or so later they embraced warmly amid the sort of sibling exchanges one would expect after such a long time apart.

Janice had been home nearly twenty-four hours and she was already experiencing the old, familiar uneasiness that was part of her South African experience. The constant feeling of awkwardness and discomfort at being waited on by servants who clearly knew their place in the scheme of things. The ever-present reminders of the structures that constituted

South African society, whether at home or out and about in Johannesburg. Above all the complacency of her family and their ingrained, subconscious attitudes of supremacy. All these strands of her white South African environment left her feeling both disappointed and disturbed. During her three years away in Israel there had been no apparent change. Yet she felt it was too early in the visit to comment and she decided to ride the situation as much as could. She had no power to change anything, nor did she want to jeopardise the ambience of her homecoming and familial reunion.

Biting her tongue did not come naturally and her efforts at restraint precipitated an uncharacteristic introversion, which initially went unnoticed.

"Everything alright darling?" Rina eventually enquired during one of several extended silences at the dinner table. "You've been home a couple of days now and we've hardly caught up with each other. "

"How are things – really?" Martin chipped in. "Are you as settled as you make out? I mean where would you say home is right now?"

"Home is where I am *based,* which right now is Israel."

"So how do you feel about coming back to your other .... your first home?" asked Rina.

"I'm not sure I want to answer that. I'm not sure I can answer that. I mean I feel ... I feel a bit_ "

"What she means is her family makes her feel uncomfortable. She doesn't approve," intervened Jonathan. He saw the look of annoyance on his sister's face. "It's true. You don't approve of us – especially me."

"Look I'm here for two weeks and I want my time to be as pleasant, as stress-free as possible," pleaded Janice. "Let's just accept we don't see things the same way, shall we?"

Janice's retort cast a pall of gloomy silence over the dinner table. When Jacob came with the main course of roast chicken and vegetables, Janice shifted uneasily in her seat, while Jonathan made a point of thanking him in a somewhat exaggerated manner.

"What's the latest with Jacob's son, Dad? asked Janice, once Jacob had left the room.

"It looks as though they'll let him out soon, but he'll have to go back."

"What'll he go back to?"

"There's a lot of money being ploughed into the Transkei you know," intervened Jonathan provocatively.

"No I didn't know! I don't see what that has to do with Joseph's problem anyway. It's a bloody disgrace!" Janice was unable to resist the bait that was dangling before her. It was a characteristic of their erratic sibling relationship. The Levy household had not resounded to such an argument for some time now and the parents caught each other's eyes knowingly.

"By the way I'm out later," said Jonathan, trying to change the topic of conversation.

"But this is our first night together as a family. I thought we could ... Where are you-?"

"I'm seeing Helen. I haven't seen her for two months now. She was away last time I was home.," said Jonathan interrupting his mother.

"Your sister's been away for three years!" snapped Martin. "The least we could expect is your first night home with *us*, with your family."

Jonathan remained silent, unwilling to make things worse. He had anticipated this problem and had delayed breaking the news. He knew his parents, and in particular his mother, disapproved of the relationship. He had tried to present his case on previous occasions, arguing their "pseudo-Jewishness" was not sufficient reason for him to narrow his selection of girlfriends. Jonathan had not set foot inside a synagogue more than three times since his barmitzvah, and they had been for family celebrations of one sort or another. He wore his surname like a badge but in every other way he did not feel Jewish nor did he identify with the usual customs and appurtenances which he regarded as part and parcel of being a member of the Jewish community in Johannesburg.

"I'll stay home tomorrow night," he said eventually. "We can have an evening of heated discussion about the politics of my country." Jonathan was unable to resist a side-swipe at his sister, whose home-coming had so far borne all the elements of a triumphant return. He could not help but feel somewhat resentful of the aura of celebrity which surrounded his sister both during her absence and more so now on her return. She had been in the Holy Land, that land which was said to be flowing with milk and honey while he had been learning to kill in the South African army near the god-forsaken town of Upington. Even her time in the army had a more glamorous context – Israel was besieged by "wicked enemies" intent on "driving her people into the Mediterranean". She was defending thousands of years of biblical heritage. Her struggle was inspirational and evocative.

Janice's absence had released Jonathan, allowing him to blossom and find more space within the family milieu. He had grown up in Janice's shadow to some extent. She had excelled at school and had she not decided to experience life on a kibbutz she would no doubt have gone to university. There was always a perception that Jonathan's mediocre performance at school would condemn him to a less than prestigious career. He had regarded school as an inconvenience rather than a stepping-stone to life as an adult. He had spent his adolescence accumulating a large circle of friends and partaking in a range of epicurean experiences which mostly filled his parents with despair. Rina had long since abandoned any pretensions to the stereotypical Jewish mother role characterised by vicarious ambition. She had come to terms with the realisation that her son's name would never be followed by a string of impressive letters and that he would have to forge for himself a meaningful existence as a working adult. Jonathan, himself, was very much a creature of the present. There was a subconscious assumption that, as a white adult, the future would resolve itself and that it was unnecessary to keep more than half an eye on what the next few years might bring.

When it had become clear to Martin that his son was not the academic sort he assumed that Jonathan would one day enter his wholesale business and ultimately take control. Jonathan had never overtly shared that assumption because he had never looked that far into his future. As yet he had shown little interest in such a career move only because he wanted to fulfil so many of his youthful needs first. Apart from his army wages he was dependent on his parents for his daily living needs. His financial situation did make for a somewhat awkward relationship with his girlfriend, Helen Peterson. He was seldom able to pay for both of them and moreover there were occasions when she ended up paying for their nights out together. To some extent this impacted on his sense of male pride as his understanding of his role in the partnership was typical of most, if not all, white South African men.

"Are we going to have the pleasure of your company at all this weekend?" asked Rina.

"I'll be home all day tomorrow as well as tomorrow night," said Jonathan.

"You don't need to do us any favours," said Janice stirring the pot of sibling rancour a little more.

"Come on you two. We don't need any of *that* behaviour this weekend" interjected Martin. "I thought you might have outgrown that sort of thing by now."

Martin's intervention was sufficient to ensure the rest of the meal was completed in silence apart from the occasional social niceties associated with table decorum.

***

The billboard announced that 'Annie Hall' was showing at 9.00 p.m. Jonathan steered Helen's Cortina into the drive-in cinema entrance. He paid the cashier and drove to the second row of cars. They were early enough to choose a good position. Jonathan got out, removed the speaker from its stand and hooked it carefully onto the window, before winding it up again so it was held in place firmly. The interior of the vehicle was to some extent isolated from the late autumn chill which had suddenly begun to make its presence felt in recent nights. It was a clear, starlit evening. The drive-in cinema was perched on top of one of Johannesburg's several mine dumps. and all around them the city lights below twinkled for miles.

"Shall we sit in the back?" asked Helen, already getting out on the passenger side. "I don't really want to end up on the gear stick!"

Jonathan chuckled and they made themselves comfortable on the back seat. Helen had taken the precaution of bringing a blanket to cover them during the film. She had brought some evening snacks and a bottle of wine. The drive-in was soon filling up steadily.

"So will I get to meet your sister?" asked Helen. "Or will that cause problems for you?"

Jonathan silenced her by pressing his lips on hers and wrapping his arms around her. Helen pulled away, removing his arm. "I asked you a question."

"I.. I don't know if there'll be time," he replied. "I have to go back to camp after this weekend and I've been asked to take part in family life."

"Meaning?"

"Meaning I'm expected to spend some time with my sister."

"But that doesn't include me." Helen's retort was more statement than question.

"You know the situation. She's been away for three years and there's a lot of catching up to be done. "

There was a brief period of silence during which Jonathan tried to resume his show of affection. But Helen was having none of it. "I don't think you understand what it's like for me, Jonnie. You come and go at my house as if you're one of us. Yet the only time I've met your parents the atmosphere was like ice."

"I know and I'm sorry. I've had countless arguments with them about their old-fashioned views of relationships. They desperately want me to marry a nice Jewish girl one day and clearly see you as some sort of threat."

"So where does that leave us? You can't honestly expect- "

"It leaves us where we want to be. I love you and I hope you love me. I'm my own person. If my folks can't come round to it then that's their problem. I don't need anyone else to tell me what to do with my life – especially my love life."

Helen pulled Jonathan towards her and kissed him. Returning the kiss, Jonathan felt the months of abstinence taking their toll. He placed a hand on her thigh under the blanket. "I want you," he mumbled through her lips.

"Well you can have me tomorrow night, my mom will be out."

"I can't see you tomorrow. I've explained."

"Well that's that then. We'll have to wait another few months."

"Don't do this to me Helen. We can go somewhere after this. Tonight. In the car."

"No thanks. We deserve more than that. *I* deserve more."

Jonathan withdrew his hand and they sat in silence for a while using the snacks as a distraction. Soon the film began, but neither was able to concentrate. Each had their own thoughts to contend with. Their year long relationship had evolved to a point where it seemed destined for something more serious. For Helen it had outgrown the awkward fumbling in cars or the snatching of odd moments at her house She wanted the physical aspect of their times together to reach a new, more elevated plane. The physical satisfaction gained by their love-making was out of kilter with her perception of what their relationship ought to be. Yes, she always wanted him physically and was usually happy to oblige when called upon, but she had always felt it was less a consummation and more a mere physical release. She wanted more normality and less snatching of moments here and there. She resented the fact that her mother was accepting of Jonathan and his background whereas she was regarded as an interloper by his parents.

After the film Helen made it clear the evening was over and after depositing Jonathan outside his house with the merest brush on his cheeks for a kiss, she drove off without a further glance at the forlorn figure standing at his garden gate.

Periods of prolonged silence had filled the time both immediately before and after the film. The drive back to Jonathan's house was particularly difficult as it was clear that Helen was not even inclined to discuss the film.

The dogs came to greet him as he entered the gate. He managed to quieten their barking and unlocked the front door as stealthily as he could. He successfully negotiated an escape to his bedroom without being accosted by either parent or his sister, who were chatting in the kitchen. He closed his bedroom door and lay on his bed in the dark.

He had looked forward to this weekend and yet, whichever way he turned, the atmosphere had been soured. Both his sister and his girlfriend had kept him at arm's length. He had another four months to go before his basic army training was finished. He had no idea what was waiting for him at the end of this period. He knew the time had come to seek greater independence and move out. The heavy hand of parental interference had become intolerable. He was becoming desperate to move to a place of his own where he could be in full control of his life. Yet to do so meant financial independence as well. He would need to get a job with sufficient income to set up his own little home. He was not sure that he was ready to share with anyone yet; the topic of moving in together had never been broached when he was with Helen.

Helen lived with her mother, Alice Peterson, a fifty-one-year-old widow. She had continued to live at home as the two women, while living independent lives, enjoyed each other's company and the house was fully paid for. Helen was in her first year as a teacher at a nearby primary school.

Helen parked her car in the driveway and sat for a while going over the unsatisfactory outcome of her only night together with Jonathan. She wondered whether it was all worth it. Snatching the odd night on his occasional sorties back home was not what she wanted at this stage of her life. Her friends led active social lives and, although they included her, she seemed to be the only one who was attached to a ball and chain. To make it worse the chain stretched as far as

Upington. For five months, she had remained faithful and steadfast in a relationship which was drifting like a clump of sargassum in danger of being washed up on the shoreline. The attitude of Jonathan's parents and his own weak reaction had not helped matters. And then of course there was the religion thing. While Jonathan had confessed to a lack of commitment to his religion, his parents had made it clear that they did not want him to have a relationship with a non-Jewish girl. Helen could not understand the meaning of 'Jew'. If he was not religious, then exactly what was it about him that could be referred to as 'Jewish'? In their many discussions about religion Jonathan had never provided a satisfactory explanation of this dichotomy. He had referred to Jews as a race as well as a religion, and had used the example of the mother's line as evidence that it went beyond mere religion. Of course, there was also the issue of a Jewish culture. Helen wasn't sure that there was anything particularly distinctive about the culture that wasn't linked directly to their religion. In what way was his South African identity so different from hers? Was there something deep-rooted in his cultural soil, which would prevent the blossoming of their relationship? When they were together there was nothing that she could detect. His surname 'Levy' was the only indication of 'otherness' about this young man she had grown so fond of in the past year. She had yet to detect a *cultural* 'otherness' which might form an impervious barrier between them.

Yet in the scheme of things the self-imposed insularity of Johannesburg Jewry reinforced the impression of a different, distinct culture, to some extent emanating from an Eastern European heritage. The Jewish community had carved out a distinctive role for itself within South Africa's white population. There were Jewish schools which not only helped to entrench religious observation but which also propagated Zionism amongst Jewish youth, ensuring Israel remained sacrosanct as the spiritual and cultural homeland of the Jewish people.

Since meeting at a mutual friend's party previously Jonathan and Helen had forged a relationship which had evolved to the stage when each had begun to contemplate a future together. Jonathan had found something comforting about being in her company. She was nearly three years older and the initial affection, mingled with respect and admiration, had become something deeper and more akin to what people called 'true love'. When in her company he felt safe and secure. The physical attraction had helped to lubricate the relationship in those inevitable, yet infrequent occasions when doubt or friction threatened.

Alice Peterson was still up and in the kitchen when her daughter entered the bungalow a short while later.

"How was your evening love?"

Helen hesitated before replying. "Okay thanks."

"Just okay. That's a pity. You haven't seen each other for a while."

"I know."

A brief period of silence followed while Helen filled the kettle.

"So what happened?" her mother persisted.

"Nothing happened. I'm just a bit fed up."

"Are you going to tell me why?"

"We had - we just had a difference – basically our relationship has hit a stumbling block."

"Do you want some Milo?"

"Thanks. A stumbling block? What do you mean?"

"We come from different backgrounds. He's Jewish and I'm not," said Helen unable to mask the annoyance in her tone.

"You don't have to define yourself by a negative, you know. You are also *something*. "

"Well at the moment I feel like a nothing. That's what I am in the eyes of his parents anyway."

"Is he religious?" asked Alice.

"No. No he's not religious."

"So what's the problem? If he's not religious I can't see why there is an issue here."

"We come from different backgrounds. His parents would rather he had a Jewish girlfriend. It's as simple as that. They see me as some sort of threat; to what, I don't understand. There's obviously something more to his Jewishness than his religion."

"I can't say I understand either," said Alice. "I know Jews tend to stick together. But what else is it that marks them out as different. I'm sure you have more in common with Jonathan than other boys you've been out with."

"Anyway I'm going to have this mug of Milo and then I'm off to bed. Good night Ma."

Alice hugged her daughter. "Good night darling. It'll sort itself out one way or another. Try to have a good night's sleep."

Helen lay awake for a while. She was coming to terms with the reality that the relationship with Jonathan would end in the near future. Perhaps it was better to end it now so she could start a new direction for her life.

***

Janice opened her eyes, awakened by the sound of a vacuum cleaner outside her room. The room was still quite dark. The clock next to the bed showed 9.30. It was a long time since she had slept so late. She got out of bed and opened the curtains, allowing the sun to flood the room.

Putting on her gown she shuffled in to the passage outside. Jacob was probing a far corner with the nozzle of the vacuum cleaner. He stopped and looked up at Janice as she hesitated outside the bathroom door.

"Good morning Jacob."

"Morning nkosazana."

Somewhat awkwardly Janice entered the bathroom and closed the door behind her. She looked into the mirror at her dishevelled hair and cheeks still creased from her pillow. Her eyes were puffy and edged with remnants of the night's sleep. There was something anomalous about sharing such intimacy with an elderly man who in many respects was a stranger, despite having worked for the Levys for such a long time.

She was no longer used to this invasion of privacy. It made her home seem more like a hotel. Her musing was interrupted by a knock on the door.

"Are you going to be long in there?" The sound of Jonathan's voice was more irritating than intrusive.

"I've only just come in!" she called.

"Bloody hell!" came the muffled reply.

Janice continued to examine the morning face before her. It was a face markedly different from those in frames scattered about the family home. The eyes had developed a cognitive window into the changes that had occurred deep within her. She had certainly matured into an independent, resilient young woman whose roots had found themselves in a new, invigorating and more fertile soil.

Having completed her ablutions and dressed, Janice made her way down to breakfast in the large Levy kitchen where Mary greeted her with a hearty chuckle. " Nkosazana ready for *big* breakfast?"

Janice reminded Mary that she was on a strict diet and suggested that a bowl of porridge would be quite sufficient. She insisted on serving herself despite Mary's protesting and exhorting her to sit at the table. Jonathan was already seated at the table and was tucking into a plate of scrambled egg on toast framed by an assortment of mushrooms, tomatoes and onions. Janice sat down opposite him and a period of silence ensued. Martin had already left for work and Rina had gone early to go the hairdresser.

It was Janice who broke the silence.

"How did last night go? Good film?"

"Uh huh. Ja good thanks."

"Am I going to get to meet your girlfriend?'

"If you want. I dunno when though. I'm going back in a couple of days."

"Why don't you invite her over tonight?"

Jonathan laughed sarcastically and continued eating.

"Why? What's the problem?" asked Janice.

"You're kidding. Can you imagine what it would be like? They can just about bear me mentioning her name."

"Oh. It's like that."

"I don't think she would come anyway. The only time they met her they made it quite clear that they didn't approve."

Janice reached a hand across the table and placed it over his. "They'll take their time, but eventually they'll come to terms with it."

"By then it'll be too late." Jonathan's sigh came from deep within.

"It's a generational thing I suppose. You and I have never had to retreat into a laager. I suppose we've never really had to put up with anti-semitism – of a serious sort anyway."

"Yeh I know," said Jonathan glumly. "It's ..... it's just so difficult to explain to Helen. It's difficult enough for me to understand."

Janice squeezed his hand before withdrawing hers. She stood up and walked to the French doors which led onto the patio. She stared out into the garden whose central feature, the swimming pool, was covered with blue plastic sheeting. The rest of the garden wore a mixture of wintry drabness interspersed with late autumn colour. "I don't miss this at all," she said without turning round. "It's really strange being back home. I didn't really know what to expect – but now I'm here I don't feel like this is home. I don't know what's going on back at real home. I haven't managed to call Yossi yet. He's been ever so busy. He works at the hospital in Jerusalem. I'm hoping he will phone tonight."

"I suppose once you've flown the nest, and tasted full independence that's it. There's no coming back."

"And you?" asked Janice. "What are your plans once the army is over?"

"I'm hoping to travel for a while. Maybe the UK. I could use it as a base for Europe."

Janice turned to face him. "And Helen?"

"Probably not. Her mother needs her to be around."

"Changing the subject," said Janice. "What about the army? How do you feel about it all? I mean do you know who your enemy is?"

"I know he's going to have a black face," said Jonathan. "I know he's somewhere in Angola, if not already in South-West Africa."

"At least I'm going to be trained to help defend my own country. I'm not sure that's the case for you."

"*Indirectly* I suppose. If they're allowed to control South-West then who's to say they won't help the ANC and the Commies for that matter?"

Mary came through from the kitchen with a plate full of toast and a cup of coffee for each of them. She collected the empty plate and bowl and placed them on the tray.

"Thanks Mary," said Janice and resumed her seat at the table. A period of silence ensued while they buttered their toast and performed the task of adding jam or marmalade accompanied by a brief exchange of pleasantries. Janice thought long and hard before her next remark, which she knew would be regarded as provocative and might possibly disrupt the smooth tenor of their conversation thus far. Nevertheless, once an idea or thought had entered her head she usually found its utterance irresistible.

"Don't let them brainwash you Jonnie."

"And your meaning?"

"I mean just because you're told that the Commies are coming to get us it doesn't necessarily mean it's true."

"I'm not sure what's worse: being brainwashed by my officers or patronised by you!" was his terse retort. Jonathan stood up and left the room.

Janice sat for a while finishing her breakfast. She knew how her brother would react but she always felt compelled to voice her opinions. Increasingly she felt isolated from her family who to all intents and purposes had remained stuck in their life patterns. She was depressed by what she perceived as the torpor which had infected their lives. Of course, they were all quite content to drift along in their cocoon of whiteness, protected from the travails, traumas and tragedies that characterized the lives of three out every four South Africans.

She thought of Jacob's son whom she had never met. A foreigner in his own country. His 'crime' was to follow in his father's footsteps to 'eGoli', the city of gold. The Transvaal was South Africa's wealthiest province. Like any young person in the world a young man in search of a better life. She imagined to a young black South African it was the commercial equivalent of the spiritual 'Aliyah' imbued in young Jews.

The sound of Jacob's vacuum cleaner starting up in the adjoining lounge signaled the end of her brief contemplation and she picked up her used crockery and cutlery and carried them through to kitchen.

***

The two men embraced on the platform. Father and son. Joseph picked up his rucksack and with a final glance at his father he boarded the train. Joseph's face soon appeared by a nearby window and as the train slowly glided out of the station the two men exchanged waves.

Jacob stood and watched the 17.55 Johannesburg to East London slowly disappear from view. His heart was laden with a mixture of sorrow and despair. Like any father, all he wanted was for his son to have the best possible opportunity in life. And clearly the best opportunities were to be found in the conurbation of the Highveld. Joseph was one of thousands of young black men who infiltrated the area illegally on a daily basis in the hope of reaping some of the rewards to be found there. For every Joseph arrested and sent back to his homeland there were at least ten more who managed to escape detection and managed to build lives for themselves. Joseph didn't know why he had been one of the unlucky ones. What had led to the late-night arrest at his friend's house? Nothing had been explained to him. It seemed likely a police informant had reported his arrival at Alexandra the previous week.

After a while Jacob left the station concourse and joined a queue at the bus terminus. He decided to spend the rest of his day off in Alexandra Township where his favourite shebeen would provide him with the necessary 'anaesthetic' to help him forget the deep pain he was feeling. He was tired of the constant setbacks, the life-long struggle to ensure the survival of his family. Amidst the loneliness of his existence in the backyard of his white employers he allowed himself the escapism of the occasional night of alcoholic over-indulgence. Yes there had been unfortunate consequences in the past and certainly much to regret each following morning; however on evenings such as this Jacob sought refuge in the hospitality of Mama Mtwetwe's powerful beer. And if the evening went well there was always the chance of a comforting embrace from either Mama Mtwetwe herself or one of the other women who hovered in the background.

The problem of transport back 'home' to the Levys soon dissipated as the alcohol took effect and Jacob was able to lose himself amongst the many souls who attended the shebeen that night.

When he was woken by Mama Mtwetwe at 4.00 a.m. the following morning, Jacob managed to gather sufficient strength to lift himself from her bed and after several attempts he was able put his trousers on, button his shirt and prepare himself for the crowded train journey which would take him to within an hour's walk from the station to the Levys' house. Through his clouded mind he knew that there would be no chance of his being on time and that he would need to not only mask the effects of his alcohol drenching but also devise a plausible explanation for yet another lateness. He had already received several warnings regarding his inability to maintain a consistent level of punctuality and the Levys appeared to be running out of tether.

It was still dark when Jacob emerged from the shebeen and joined the steady stream of people making their way to the Alexandra station about two kilometres away. Although his head was aching it wasn't long before the crisp early morning air began to clear his brain and as he walked he began to formulate the excuse which he hoped would prove sufficiently convincing to his employers.

He would say that Joseph's train had been cancelled and they had spent the night in Alexandra in the hope that he might catch the scheduled morning train. He had tried to phone the Levys but the only call box he could find was not working. Nice and simple. Plausible.

***

Martin didn't buy the excuse. In recent years he had grown to recognise the signs on Jacob's face. Sporadic bouts of heavy drinking had vandalised Jacob's visage with increasingly puffed skin around the eyes and an ever-spreading network of veins in the whites of both. Jacob had developed a morose demeanour not unlike that to be found on the old boxer dog stretched out on the kitchen floor that morning.

Nevertheless, as usual, Martin found it convenient to overlook the lateness of Jacob's arrival in the Levy household that morning – as he had done on numerous occasions in the past. It was easier. Short of making Jacob's drinking a sackable offence there was little he felt he could do. And to sack him, particularly in the light of the latest problem, would have been more than he was able to countenance. Besides, Jacob had apologised profusely, as usual – and the apology was accompanied by the inevitable promise never to repeat the offence.

Martin had his own son's impending departure on his mind that morning. He hated the prospect of saying goodbye yet again. He had learnt to shut out the image of his son standing on a deserted rural stretch of road hitchhiking back to camp. He had learnt to put to one side the thought of his learning to become a soldier, a killer of men. And of course now, in addition, he had to come to terms with the image of his daughter dressed in Israeli military uniform. Warfare had skipped a generation in Martin's case. His own father had seen service in the North African desert in the early 1940s, but Martin himself had just missed out. Now both his children had found themselves in conflict zones.

The likelihood of Jonathan seeing service in South West Africa was increasing by the day. Aside from South African forces having to deal with SWAPO insurgents it had been decided to launch a pre-emptive offensive into Angola itself. So the chance of Jonathan becoming actively involved in border operations was more a matter of 'when' than 'if'.

The family farewell that morning had an added poignancy. Brother and sister had no idea when they would see each other again. Their reunion had gone relatively well but the realisation that a gulf between them had opened in recent years had left regrets likely to fester for some time.

To make the departure more bearable, Martin had insisted that Jonathan take a bus to Upington where he was to meet a friend who had offered him a lift to camp. The journey was well over eight hundred kilometres and he would be spending the whole day on the bus.

***

The motion of the bus induced a brief slumber as Jonathan left the Witwatersrand for the open country. It hadn't been a particularly productive weekend back home, as his personal relationships with both girlfriend and family had remained largely unresolved. He was left with a deep sense of unfulfillment which, coupled with the uncertain short-term future direction of his army training, made his departure that morning more uncomfortable than usual. Saying goodbye to his sister was particularly discomfiting as there was so much that had been left in the air. Apart from the physical distance between them there appeared to be little now that bound them beyond the usual familial ties which their parents had so assiduously attempted to maintain, but to little avail. Rina, in particular, had urged brother and sister to maintain a sense of familial decorum and mutual respect, even if sibling love was apparently out of the question.

The seat next to Jonathan had been empty and, determined to keep it unoccupied, he had placed his bag there as a statement to other passengers. However the bus soon filled up and when it stopped to pick up a lone passenger at Lichtenburg, Jonathan reluctantly removed the bag from the only vacant seat and placed it on the rack above him. A slenderly-built man in his early to mid thirties and wearing a pale green safari suit took the seat beside him. His cursory good morning was followed by a minute or so of fidgeting while he made himself as comfortable as possible in a seat which was, admittedly, insufficiently padded.

"Sorry about that," said his neighbour. "no better than my garden bench."

"Jonathan half grunted, half chuckled. He had detected a trace of an English accent without being able to locate its origin more accurately.

His neighbour was now rummaging in a large shopping bag and, eventually retrieving a copy of that morning's Rand Daily Mail, he began to scour the back sports page as if searching for a number in the telephone directory.

"Can't find anything," he grunted in disgust. "Nothing about the weekend's football results. I don't suppose you know how Chelsea did on Saturday. Home match against Wolves. "

"No – sorry!" Jonathan wasn't sure he wanted to pursue this opening conversational gambit, lest it led to something more substantial. All he wanted now was to sleep; something he had been unable to achieve to any significant extent during his weekend at home.

"You a football man?" The man was determined to engage.

"No rugby."

"Do you play?" There was no escape now. Jonathan was obliged to answer and so signal to his companion that a conversational rally was underway.

"Not at the moment. I was in my school's first fifteen."

" Oh what school was that?"

"I went to King David – er King David Victory Park. There are two King Davids in Jo'burg. There's also Linksfield."

"Yes ..... King David." Jonathan's companion fell silent for a while. The bus was on a long straight road lined with seemingly endless flat farmland on either side. Jonathan decided to close his eyes and let the motion of the bus do its job.

"So apart from the obvious, what do you do to keep fit these days?" The man was determined to pursue a conversation.

"Mainly volleyball in the army," came the reply with just a hint of irritation at having to respond.

"So how long have you got to go?"

"Only a couple of months now."

"And then? What have you got lined up?"

"Nothing yet." Jonathan didn't feel like asking any questions himself. A further spell of silence ensued and he managed to doze awhile.

He woke when the bus stopped in Vryburg. Two middle-aged women got off and were replaced by a young couple. Jonathan rummaged in his bag for beef and tomato sandwiches, which Mary had prepared that morning. His companion was perusing a brochure, so Jonathan decided not to disturb him.

"Diamonds. I'm in diamonds. I'm on my way to Upington for a couple of days and then back to Cape Town."

Jonathan was slightly taken aback at this unsolicited announcement. The man next to him was obviously anxious to ensure they conversed for the majority of the remaining leg of their journey. Nevertheless, his curiosity *was* now aroused and he wondered why this man was on a bus making a long distance journey when he was clearly in a position to be either driving himself or even flying across the country engaging in diamond transactions.

"Have you caught this bus before?" asked Jonathan, feeling obliged to say something.

"No," came the reply accompanied by a chuckle. "I've got a driving ban for the next twelve months. I had a bit too much drink at my friend's wedding and made the mistake of driving home. I would've been okay if I hadn't collided with a lamppost. Car was a write-off. Apparently I could hardly talk to the police when they arrived on the scene. So here I am."

Another period of silence followed. The man started tapping something apparently tuneless on the armrest between their seats. Eventually Jonathan decided he needed to say something.

"Are you from the UK?"

"Yes indeed I am. Originally from Reading .... Berkshire, then a few years in London until I was offered a contract out here. Once the contract was up I joined a local export company. SA Gems Ltd. Heard of them?"

"No – not my field really."

"We export rough diamonds to the UK and the rest of Europe. I've been here six years now. Love it. Best thing that's ever happened to me. A way of life you can only dream about in England."

Jonathan couldn't think of anything to say in response and a brief spell of silence ensued.

"Frank Dickinson by the way." His companion thrust his right hand in front of Jonathan, taking him somewhat by surprise.

"Oh yes – Jonathan Levy." Jonathan shook the proffered hand firmly.

"Pleased to meet you Jonathan. You guys are doing a great job on our behalf. If it wasn't for you this country would be run by commies. Look at the rest of this continent. Can you name one stable country north of Rhodesia and South-West? ...... There isn't one. This country is Africa's treasure house. It needs to remain that way – by force if necessary. Levy eh? Nice Jewish name."

"Yes." Jonathan detected a faintly derisory tone in the comment. He decided to give Dickinson the benefit of the doubt but even so it left him feeling a little uncomfortable. He looked out the window as if to indicate he wanted to be left alone. There was still no change to the endless flat landscape occasionally punctuated by a lone tree or homestead.

"I'm back in the UK for two weeks next Friday. Different landscape altogether."

"I've never been." Jonathan's gaze remained steadfastly on the passing scenery.

"Any plans to go?"

"Not in the immediate future. Hopefully once my army training is over I'll get a chance to travel."

Jonathan's recounting of the next few minutes included the screeching of tyres, several screams, his head crashing against the window of the bus and then onto the back of the seat in front. He remembered the body of another passenger, no doubt Dickinson, hitting his shoulder and then a silence.

Jonathan was able to extricate himself from the tangle of arms and legs and stood up. The driver had left his seat and was already making his way along the aisle, checking on the well-being of his passengers. Dickinson gave a groan and managed to right himself in his seat. Jonathan saw that his forehead was bleeding. Her passed a handkerchief to Dickinson.

"That's a nasty gash. Put your head back and hold this tight on the wound."

Dickinson winced as he placed the handkerchief on his forehead. It seemed his forehead had hit the ashtray on the back of the seat in front of Jonathan.

The bus had apparently swerved off the road and had come to rest, upright, half in a ditch at the side.

"Everybody okay?" The driver's voice quivered half –heartedly, barely audible. "Those of you who can should try to leave the bus". He had managed to restore a semblance of authority to his voice. "There's an emergency door at the back. Anyone injured?"

Jonathan raised his hand and pointed to his companion. "He's got a head wound – bleeding a lot."

"Can he get off? Can you help him?" asked the driver.

Jonathan encouraged Dickinson to stand and join the slow queue of passengers making its way to the front exit.

One by one the passengers stepped onto the grass verging the field. Apart from one elderly woman and to some extent Dickinson, all the passengers were able to leave independently. She required support but was able to shuffle to the step where Jonathan and another young man carried her from the bus.

An elderly black woman was sitting in the ditch about thirty metres further back from the bus. Her right arm appeared broken and blood was seeping through her dress near her shoulder. Clearly in shock she sat staring at the bus in silence.

The driver approached her, accompanied by some of the passengers. "I swerved at the last minute," he muttered. "Just caught her and then lost control."

"They *will* walk on the road side," said a woman passenger. "They never think of walking against the traffic."

Meanwhile the driver of a passing Toyota sedan had stopped and come over to investigate. "Can I do anything? What's happened?"

"One passenger injured. He's going to need an ambulance. If you wouldn't mind calling for one when you reach the next town please. This girl is injured. I think she's going to need treatment," said the bus driver. "Maybe you can send for one to fetch her as well. We also need to contact the bus company and let them know what's happened."

"Okay. I'm on my way to Schweizer-Reneke. I'll sort out something when I get there." The bus driver jotted down some details on paper and handed it to the man. He hurried towards his car and drove off immediately.

Jonathan squatted down beside the injured woman who hardly noticed him. "Are you okay?" he asked in a low voice .

There was no immediate response but eventually she answered hoarsely, "Yes master. Okay."

"Can you stand?" asked Jonathan.

Without talking she tried to stand using her left arm as a lever. A male passenger had come over to find out what the problem was. "She's drunk," he observed. "Look at her. Look at her eyes."

"She's been hit by a bus. She's in shock," said Jonathan curtly. He didn't look up as he continued supporting the woman. She managed to stand independently. She walked slowly towards a large brightly coloured bag lying on the verge. Some of its contents, an assortment of rags and plastic bags, had spilled out. Slowly she bent down to retrieve them.

At that moment another vehicle drew up, stopping behind the bus. A man got out and came over to investigate.

"Is everyone okay here? Can I help? I am a doctor," announced the bespectacled man dressed in a brown suit.

The driver of the bus took charge and guided the man towards Dickinson who was sitting on a suitcase beside the bus. His forehead had been bandaged with a towel. The doctor proceeded to dress the wound with a proper bandage.

"Hopefully an ambulance will be along soon," said the bus driver.

"That's good. He should be okay for a while," said the doctor. Anyone else?"

"Yes, a woman was knocked over by the bus. I think she's broken her arm and her shoulder is bleeding," said Jonathan.

He turned to where he had left her but she had disappeared. Jonathan ran round to the front of the bus to look for her. She was nowhere to be seen. She wasn't anywhere along the grass verge or even in the field beside the road. Nor was she across the road. She had slipped away from the scene unnoticed.

An hour or so later an ambulance arrived and Dickinson was taken off to hospital in Vryburg, a town dome twenty kilometres away. The elderly lady had been checked over by the ambulance crew and appeared fit enough to continue her journey. Another coach soon arrived on the scene and the rest of the passengers boarded and were soon on their way again.

Jonathan wondered what became of the woman who disappeared. She had clearly been injured to the extent that she needed treatment. Her arm had appeared broken and who knew what other damage she had suffered. Even so she appeared to have been forgotten and was not mentioned again.

***

Rina parked the car and a short while later mother and daughter entered the large Sandton shopping mall. The mission was to ensure that Janice's spare suitcase was well stocked with all her clothing needs for the coming Jerusalem winter. Rina had missed her daughter during the last three years and merely to go shopping together was a treat she had been anticipating with considerable pleasure. On the other hand Janice had acquired an aversion to such shopping expeditions and had demonstrated little enthusiasm for the trip to Sandton. She regarded Sandton's huge shopping centre as an example of the sort of cocoon within which South Africa's whites encased themselves.

The two women decided that tea would be a good idea to begin with and they found a corner of a café which advertised a range of 'home-baked' cakes, scones and buns.

"Will it ever change here?" came Janice's first salvo. "I've been away three years and everything in this land has stood still."

Rina looked down, unwilling to make eye contact with her daughter. She always felt uncomfortable when discussing politics. There was an inevitability about the direction of this impending discourse. Deep down Rina knew her daughter was right. Although Janice always managed to find the most vulnerable spot of her complacency, Rina half admired her daughter's propensity for provocation.

"Change darling? What change were you expecting?" came the response, not without a contrived insouciance.

"Attitude . A change in attitude for starters," said Janice. "It was only a couple of years ago that Soweto up. I expected *something* to have changed. Surely something had to give."

"Nothing happens overnight, darling. In fact, you could argue Soweto, you know the whole Afrikaans language business, was a setback as far as the blacks were concerned. They may have shot themselves in the foot. They provoked the Afrikaner so much that he withdrew into his laager."

"They, they, they! That's all I hear. *They* do this and *they* do that. It's never we or us," snorted Janice. " This country has no hope as long it's *them* and *us*. That's the difference in Israel. Everyone I meet or have anything to do with is on the same side. Everyone in Israel has something in common. Their religion – their heritage!" Rina put her hand on Janice's as if to pacify her. It was a maternal gesture whose message was *I don't really want to continue this lest it take us down the usual path of acrimony and ultimate regret.*

Janice however ignored the signal. She was all too aware of her surroundings. An upmarket shopping mall, sanitised by its *all-whiteness.* The only black faces belonged to cleaners or waiters. Occasionally a domestic servant in uniform accompanied her 'madam' as parcel carrier to the car. Her sense of justice forced her to carry on.

"I hate this," she continued. "It should be normal. Me here in this environment. But it isn't. It's far from normal. Israel is my new normal. There's another world out there mom. South Africans, and by that I mean white South Africans, need to sort out their minds. They need to sort out their attitudes. They can't go on like this living in cloud cuckoo land-"

"Why cloud cuckoo land?"

"It's not real - all this. It's not normal to get up in the morning and have my breakfast served by someone who lives in my backyard. Someone who has watched me grow up, who knows me almost as well as you do but can't even sit down with me and have a cup of tea with me. It's abnormal. And I want normality when I come back home. Home? Is this home? I don't even know that for sure any more."

It was as if Rina was stunned into silence by the diatribe. The two women sat sipping their tea without making eye contact. Janice stared at the passing human traffic, unable to avoid the gnawing unease inside. She watched a smartly dressed middle aged white woman, adorned with an array of expensive jewellery and hair neatly styled, stop and peer into a clothing shop window displaying incongruously garish

SALE signs. Eventually temptation appeared to triumph over discretion and the woman strode purposefully into the store.

"Every country has its issues. Or its problems." Rina broke the silence. "Your father and I often wonder whether Israel is the answer to the Jews' problems."

"What problems?"

"The problems of centuries in the Diaspora. It's wonderful that we all have a homeland that we can turn to if necessary. It's such a tiny country I wonder whether it could cope if we all suddenly decided to live there."

"I can't see that happening." Janice finished her tea and wiped her mouth. " There are too many Jews in the States who would never take the plunge. Too many living here and in Europe. Life in Israel is no bed of roses. It's as tough as anywhere. It's a far more attractive proposition for wealthy American Jews or those living here for that matter to make their donations and continue their standard of living. I mean the average Israeli is reasonably comfortable. Don't get me wrong. It's not the third world. But it can be a struggle and of course there's always the physical danger ... the possibility of another war around the corner. It's only four years ago the future of Israel was on a knife-edge. The Yom Kippur War wasn't the trouncing of 67. It's likely to be even more difficult in the future."

"I know what you mean darling. Your father and I are too settled here to contemplate upping sticks and starting a new life; whether in Israel or anywhere else for that matter. I will admit we are entrenched in our way of life here. You are young. You have the energy, the drive and the ... yes, I suppose, the principles needed to do what you are doing. "

"It's never too late to do what's right Mom. It's never too late."

"Don't forget your dad and I love this country. This is my home. Okay I came here as a very young girl but in my mind this is home – my homeland. I'm a patriot."

"Whatever that means," said Janice unable to disguise the hint of disdain in her tone.

"It's a feeling I'm sure. I can't rationalise it. It's not up here, it's here in my heart."

Janice looked skeptical. "What part of being South African appeals to you? Is it the landscape? Is it the people? "

"Both."

"Why did I know you would say that? Which people? Is it Mary or Jacob? Is it Jacob's son, a foreigner in his own country? What makes a person a South African? Or should we have different types, different classes of South African? Who would represent the typical South African to people overseas? Of course, you are unlikely to bump into a black South African overseas. There are very few who could afford an overseas trip."

"I've just said you can't rationalise these things. It's what you feel for the whole package that makes up the country South Africa."

"But that's the difference. I can rationalise it. I *can* rationalise my commitment to Israel. It makes sense for Jews to regard Israel as their homeland. There's always been a historical attachment to Israel, Canaan or whatever it might have been called. The UN itself was able to rationalise it by granting the land to the Jews."

"Janice Levy! I can't believe it! When did you get back?" The voice belonged to a short, smartly dressed young woman, heavily made-up with long dark hair draped across each shoulder.

"Moira! My God! How *are* you? " Janice leapt up and embraced her best friend from her school days at King David in Linksfield.

The girls drew apart and studied each other. "When did you get back? Are you here for good?"

Janice shook her head. "I'm back for a couple of weeks to see the family," she said, acknowledging her mother's presence.

"Hello Mrs Levy. Nice to see you," said Moira.

"And you too," said Rina. "Sit down and join us. Would you like a cup of tea?"

"Sorry I can't. I've got to rush. Why don't you come over later, Jan? Justin will be there. He's... he's been away ... He'd love to see you."

"So much has happened since...." Janice hesitated.

"I know, but you both need to put that behind you. Justin often talks about how much he regrets - but anyway enough of that, come over tomorrow. Come and have tea with us."

Janice looked at her mother for a sign of approval. Instead she received a quizzical look on Rina's face, which she interpreted as "It's your life you're old enough to do as you want."

"I'd love to. Thank you," she said with minimal deliberation.

"Wonderful! Come at about three. See you then." The two young women brushed each other's cheeks and Moira left.

***

Moira Greenspan lived with her parents in a large double-storey house in one of the most exclusive roads of Rosebank. It was set in an expansive garden immaculately manicured and maintained by a head gardener in charge of a team of three. A line of stinkwood trees stood to attention on either side of the long meandering driveway which led from the security gates to the large parking area fronting the main entrance to the house.

Janice parked her mother's Ford Anglia behind one of the closed garage doors and rang the front door bell. A few seconds later a tall good-looking young man with close-cropped, almost black hair opened the door.

"Justin Greenspan!" Janice and Justin embraced.

"You look good. Obviously life in Israel suits you."

"I can't complain. It's my home now. What happened to that lovely long shoulder length hair?"

"Well it's a long story which I'll tell you later. Let's say the warders didn't appreciate it." This comment was accompanied by a wry smile. "Come through."

The large entrance hall provided a choice of four doors, one of which led through to the large living room, where Justin's father was reading that morning's edition of The Citizen. Harvey Greenspan rose from his chair to greet Janice with an affectionate hug. "You look wonderful! Positively blooming. That Israeli sunshine obviously agrees with you."

"Thank you," replied Janice. "It's lovely to see you again."

"Come through to the patio," said Justin. "Moira won't be long. She and my mom have gone to have their hair done. I'm actually just visiting. I'm living with a group of friends in Hillbrow. Let me get you something to drink. Coke? Lemonade?"

"A glass of lemonade would be great thanks."

Janice went out onto the patio. She gazed across the expanse of lawn stretching beyond the mandatory swimming pool in the foreground. The lawn was bordered by a collection of exotic plants against a backdrop of tall trees.

Justin returned with a tray of drinks and biscuits. "Yes I should explain. I've been in prison for six months."

"Oh!" Janice was taken aback by the suddenness of this declaration. Clearly her parents had blanked all news of this in their letters. Rina, in particular, preferred not to mention his name, let alone reveal that her ex-boyfriend had been arrested, lest it evoke feelings of sympathy within her daughter.

"Yep. Six months. My new badge of honour," said Justin, smiling weakly. "That's where membership of a banned organisation gets you."

"What do your parents say?" asked Janice.

"They are not keen to have their good name besmirched. They've had their fill of Special Branch crawling all over the house, rifling through my dad's desk and the rest. I imagine they're also embarrassed."

"Moira?"

"Moira's not quite sure how to react. On one level she's rather proud of her brother. Dare I say almost a case of reflected glory. On the other hand the name Greenspan now carries a different sort of baggage. She's had journalists hounding her, even accusing her of being a member of the ANC. My sister likes to keep her head down and get on with living the life of a young white Jewish woman in Jo'burg."

"Well that's what I am!" Moira stepped onto the patio. "I'm so pleased you could make it Jan. So, what do you think of my brother? A young man with a record."

Janice stood up to greet Moira. "Actually I admire him. I wish I had the guts …"

"Anyway I'll leave you two to catch up with each other's news," said Justin, standing immediately. "I've got some catching up of my own to do. Hopefully see you before you go Jan."

"That would be nice," said Janice.

"I'll ring you."

Justin left and the two young women sat in the warm Johannesburg late autumn sunshine.

"Actually I'm worried about him," said Moira. "He had a really tough time inside. They put him through hell to get what they wanted. It seems he was broken eventually. That's why he's out three months early."

"That's terrible!" said Janice, her mind going back to the days when they were together. Ultimately she and Justin had had a difference of opinion about the best way to further their political idealism. She had been content to work for Helen Suzman at election time. She would either canvas, help put up campaign posters or on election day offer her services in whatever capacity she was needed.

Justin had been very critical of her alignment with the Progressives' cause. He saw it as rather pointless. Indeed, he had become angry one evening while they were enjoying a meal together in a Hillbrow café, when she had spoken in favour of their policy of a qualified franchise. That evening appeared to be the trigger for their relationship to become increasingly strained until ultimately their times together were no longer mutually fulfilling. Justin was becoming obsessed with his involvement in the ANC struggle and every waking moment appeared dedicated to that cause. Anyone who was out of kilter with his politics was unlikely to play a significant role in his life. So gradually Janice found herself being squeezed out of Justin's immediate sphere of influence. They saw less and less of each other until the bond was finally fractured.

Martin and Rina were relieved when he no longer visited and moreover delighted when their daughter had clearly broken the relationship once and for all.

"That boy will bring you nothing but heartache," Rina had said on more than one occasion. "Once he becomes involved with Special Branch, BOSS or whoever. You don't want to be sucked into his problems."

"My parents are at their wits end," said Moira. " My dad is doing his best to get him back on an even keel. He has managed to arrange a trial period selling motor spares for a wholesaler friend of his. Do you remember Leibowitz and Son in Randberg?"

"No. It doesn't ring a bell."

"My dad's friend Joe Leibowitz is prepared to give Justin a chance. Good of him as I don't think he needs extra staff."

"I still can't get over how they treated Justin," said Janice. "It's really disturbing that they can break somebody down like that. I always thought Justin was quite strong - mentally tough."

"Well it appears he is more brittle than we thought. I don't think he is a member of the ANC any longer. He told my parents that his days of being an activist are finished." Moira was keen to change the subject, which had been such a festering sore for her family for the past few months. "Anyway I want to hear about you. Tell me how things are for you in Israel."

The maid came out with a tray of tea and cake at that point. Janice didn't recognise her and stood up to introduce herself. It turned out that Mary and this woman Grace were good friends. They attended the same church on Sundays.

"Israel is wonderful," said Janice. "I just feel so at home there. I would love you to come over and spend some time with me. You would love it. It's just such a vibrant country. Young and modern but surrounded by so much ancient history."

"I hope I'll be able to come and visit you soon. I've got lots of travel plans now that I've graduated. As for Aliyah .... that could be a step too far. I'm not sure." Moira poured the tea and handed her friend a cup and a slice of sponge cake.

"Thanks. I always thought the best way to shake off the after-effects of Zionist brainwashing I received at school would be to go to Israel and get it out of my system once and for all," said Janice.

"It obviously didn't work," said Moira.

"No it didn't. Within a few weeks I was as passionately patriotic as any Sabra."

"So instead of getting it out of your system it got well and truly into your system."

"You could say that. So, what about you? How do you see your future?"

Moira took a few seconds to answer while she finished her tea. "I've hit a bit of a snag. I've met a medical student from Cape Town....."

"And? Tell me more," said Janice. "What's he like?"

"Well.. he's kind, he's generous, he's considerate."

"And? Is he the one?"

"I think so. In fact, I'm pretty sure." Moira reached into her bag and drew out a photograph.

"This is Sol. What do you think?"

"Impressive. He has a kind face as well as being good-looking. So, where does this leave your plans?"

"A bit up in the air at the moment. Now that I'm a qualified teacher, if I want, there's a job waiting at King David Victory Park in January next year."

"And Sol?"

"Sol has four more years to go. That's a bit of a complication. I'd like to travel. Although it means we will spend a long time apart, it'll be a good test for our relationship."

"Where do you think you'll go? Hopefully Israel for some of the time at least."

"I'm sure Israel will be on the itinerary. It's what we do as Jews. Jews go to Israel. It's a bit like a pilgrimage I suppose. That doesn't mean we have to live there."

"No of course it doesn't. I can't say why I feel so at home and so patriotic towards Israel. Is it something spiritual? I don't know. All I know is that from the time I arrived I felt I belonged. Even though I only had a smattering of Hebrew – (if you remember we both did badly in matric), I still fitted in and was accepted immediately. In some ways it was rather weird; everyone from street sweepers and window cleaners to judges and doctors was a Jew. Yes, the so-called chosen people are represented across Israeli society. Even the burglars are Jewish!"

Moira nodded in acknowledgement. "I know it's strange. I remember my first visit overseas. To see white people doing menial jobs like cleaning windows and sweeping streets was almost shocking. It took me a while to get used to it!"

"Well we do have quite a sheltered existence in this part of the world. One day that will all change and I only hope the whites in this country will be ready when it happens."

Moira remained silent. Politics had become a painful subject for her and she preferred to avoid any such discussion.

***

"It's Justin for you," said Rina, unable to hide the annoyance in her voice.

Janice picked up the phone in the hallway. Justin wanted to take her for dinner. She reassured her mother that the gap between them, which had widened since her absence, was unbridgeable and she had no need to worry. Besides she had someone else now.

There was something different about the Justin she had encountered at his parents' house the previous day. His eyes were almost lifeless, lacking the sparkle of a young man who had a reputation as a firebrand, a political hothead who exuded confidence in his own opinions and his desire to change the country, if not the world. A young man who didn't allow personal relationships to interfere with his wider political goals, which had become all consuming. Janice was keen to explore further the reasons behind the transformation in his demeanour. What had happened during the weeks he had spent in prison to distil an unrecognisable meekness and newly found propensity for social niceties? The former version of Justin had regarded these as unnecessary and likely to inhibit the zeal and passion required to confront the system. Moreover, there was no room for subtlety as a tactical ingredient of 'the struggle'. Justin had some awareness for the distaste his parents had for his "political shenanigans". However, after a period during which they had humoured him in the hope he would soon come to his senses, they had lost patience with his intolerance and stubbornness in the face of a government determined to confront opposition with the most ferrous of fists. They had argued that Justin was being used by the ANC. "A pawn rather than a knight or a bishop," his father had said. He was being used and, if necessary, the ANC would dump him as an expendable element of the struggle.

Even so Justin believed he had a meaningful role within the organisation. Active politics gave him an adrenalin rush unmatched by any other activity he had experienced. There was something exciting about the illicit nature of what he regarded as "true opposition politics". None of the anodyne even pointless opposition exemplified by Helen Suzman and her followers. The 'Progs' as they were known could spend the rest of their lives indulging in activities regarded by the ANC as the 'meaningless trappings and associated frippery' of all-white South African election campaigns.

"I'll fetch at you at eight tomorrow night," said Justin. "Are you okay with a steak house? There's a Steers just opened in Sandton."

"That sounds good. See you tomorrow at eight."

***

The steak house was full of diners and Janice and Justin had to wait twenty minutes for a table. Competition to be heard in the restaurant was keen and the noise level had steadily increased while they waited. Although Justin clearly knew a large number of people only one or two managed more than a brief greeting or cursory wave from the other side of the room. It was evident that people were reluctant to be associated with a young man whose trial had featured prominently in the Johannesburg news pages for weeks earlier in the year. Members of a group at a nearby table were pleased to see Janice, but eschewed the opportunity to engage with her for more than a few moments. The waiting period accentuated the awkwardness of the moment. It became easier when they were eventually seated at a table in a corner where they could face each other and shut themselves off from the rest of the restaurant.

"I still can't get used to this," said Janice studying the menu.

"Meaning?"

"Meaning the all-whiteness of places like this. We are in Africa for God's sake!"

"You grew up with it."

"Three years away from it have changed the way I view normality."

"I know. It's difficult to believe we're in 1978," said Justin. "It's strange being part of it. I think you did the right thing."

"*You* did the right thing. The courageous thing that's for sure."

"Courageous? Do you really think so?"

"I do," said Janice. "I'm not sure I could do the same. It takes a lot of courage to confront this government, let alone the establishment."

The waiter whom Janice recognised from her schooldays arrived to take their order. He cast a brief glance at Justin with undisguised disdain and then proceeded to ignore him. They ordered their wine and food, with the waiter clearly intent on communicating only with Janice.

"There are many people who regard me as a traitor." Justin looked away avoiding eye contact with Janice. She saw his eyes glistening as they welled up.

"What's the matter?" asked Janice. "What is it Justin?" She placed a hand on his and squeezed it gently.

For a few moments he said nothing, unable to look at her. Then he wiped his eyes and faced her again.

"I'm no hero Jan. I.. I've let people down. "

"What do you mean?"

Justin hesitated before replying. "I've sold out."

"What do you mean 'sold out'? " Janice removed her hand from his and rummaged through her bag for a cigarette. She offered one to Justin and lit both. Justin drew long and hard before continuing.

"I sang like the proverbial canary. ....you know .... a .. grass." He saw the shock on Janice's face and hesitated for a few moments before continuing. "When I was in prison I was ..." Again his eyes filled with tears. Janice did not recognise this man sitting before her. Always so sure of himself. Always ready to shoot down the opinions of others. Now he was a broken man unable to make prolonged eye contact nor stem the flow of tears that continued to fill his eyes.

"What do you mean? What about when you were in prison?" intervened Janice.

" They made me .... they made me talk." Again Justin's eyes filled.

Janice took his hand again and squeezed gently.

"You mean tortured you?" she said.

"Yes tortured. I was kept in isolation without proper lighting for the first week. I lost track of the time. I had no watch."

"Justin this is awful. I can't believe it!"

"They wouldn't let me sleep. They kept coming in and waking me."

"The bastards!"

"There's worse. One of them kicked me repeatedly until I gave names."

"Kicked you?"

"Yeah in the balls and, when I fell to the ground, in my stomach; on my back. This happened every day until I gave in."

"Did you have access to a lawyer?"

"Not for the first week. Only when I started to crumble and give them what they wanted."

"Is there more Jus? Did they do anything else to you?"

"The worst thing-" Justin hesitated. "The worst thing was the way they twisted my mind. They manipulated my thoughts all the while this was going on." Justin stopped. The waiter arrived with their wine.

When the waiter left, Justin continued. "Did you know I turned state witness? I betrayed my comrades, my movement ...... ultimately I betrayed my country."

Janice didn't respond. Justin had been reduced to a relative weakling, a feeble residue of the man she had once regarded as her soul mate. What disturbed her more was the idea that he was despised by both sides now.

Once the meal was underway there was a prolonged period of silence punctuated by brief exclamations in praise of the steak, the salad and cabernet sauvignon. She felt pity for this man who had been reduced to a nonentity, both political and social, by a cruel regime. But what was now clear was the sheer irrelevance of ordinary white so-called activists across the opposition political spectrum. Unless you were prepared to stand up to the regime and suffer the consequences you were doomed to irrelevance or even worse reduced to the pathetic figure in front of her now. It took whites of special courage and resolve, like Ruth First and Joe Slovo to have the long-term staying power to be integral parts of the movement. Even so, more often than not, they had to operate outside South Africa in order to play a meaningful role. Either that or they ended up in prison.

"You said they twisted your mind. What do you mean? How did they twist your mind?" she asked eventually.

"They befriended me. Once I caved in .." Justin stopped as if horrified by his own description. "Once I decided to give them what they wanted, they changed their tune completely. They went out of their way to treat me well. I was given special privileges. I was allowed to watch television in my cell. I was allowed to read acceptable novels. I was well fed and even treated to the occasional beer. Certain individuals would come to my cell for a chat. Slowly but surely they ingratiated themselves. By the time of the trial they were my mates. They looked out for me, they gave me encouragement. And do you know I still get visits! They treat me like I'm their 'maat'. They claim they are looking out for me 'cause I could be a victim of a revenge attack."

"Have you felt threatened?"

"No just ostracised. I'm not sure which is worse."

"Whose trial was it?"

"David Bernstein. My lecturer at varsity. He was arrested at the same time as me. I had no contact with him at all. They saw him as a vital cog in the wheel. He was the one .. it was because of me that...." Justin hesitated for a few moments composing himself once more. "I was a witness for the state at his trial."

"Where is he now?" asked Janice.

"He is somewhere in the Cape. He was found guilty of terrorist activities under the Internal Security Act. He would probably be there anyway, but ... but I didn't help. So my dear Jan you are looking at a coward."

"Don't be hard on yourself Jus. You aren't cruel. You've never tortured anybody and never could. Most people would have reacted the way you did. Most of those people who judge you haven't been in a similar situation themselves."

"The worst thing about this is I've lost my self-respect. No one can be loved or respected by everybody. But at the very least you should be able to respect yourself."

Justin lit up another cigarette during the brief period of silence which followed. Janice affected the need to rummage through her bag for some mints although she knew there were none there. When their eyes met again she leant forward, elbows on the table, resting her chin on her hands.

"So what next for Justin Greenspan? What's he going to do with his life?"

"I don't know. I'm tempted to leave the country and start up somewhere new. Maybe the UK. My father was born in London, so I could move there."

"Have you been to England?"

"Only once. I liked what I saw. The language of course is an important factor. The freedom to have your say. The political spectrum allows for the full range of ideologies."

"Have you got family there?"

"My father has a cousin who lives in Exeter. Far from London, but nevertheless a contact at least."

Justin's father had spent the first five years of his life in England before his parents decided to emigrate to what they perceived as a land of opportunity. His parents were migrants from Lithuania and after almost ten years in England they had made little progress in adapting to life there.

"Anyway," continued Justin, "I still have a lot of thinking and weighing up to do. My parents are obviously keen for me to get back on my feet and do something with my life here. Of course, I never did finish my politics degree. I've only got one year left and I have to decide what to do on that front. Not sure it'll get me on my feet financially. I also need my independence. Living back at home isn't exactly progress. Fortunately I've managed to get a room with some guys in Hillbrow now. But it's only a short-term arrangement."

"Ever thought of going to Israel?" asked Janice. "Maybe that's an option worth thinking about."

"Not sure that's my scene really. You know, the whole political background – the fact that a version of apartheid exists there –"

"Apartheid? That's a bit of an exaggeration," interjected Janice, a hint of anger in her voice.

"I was brainwashed at school; as you probably were. You know, the whole Six Day War thing and then of course the Yom Kippur War. I only ever got one version of events; one version of the reasons for those wars. The whole conflict since '48 in fact." A smidgen of the erstwhile passionate campaigner was briefly evident in Justin's tone.

"The minute I entered the country I felt I was at home," said Janice. "A wonderful feeling of camaraderie, of belonging. Now I can't see myself living anywhere else. You could walk in tomorrow and immediately become an Israeli citizen."

"By a quirk of fate?"

"Look we've, the Jews I mean, have been running for years. Ever since we left Egypt with Moses in charge. It's about time we settled in the promised land."

"I wish I could buy into all that Old Testament business. It would be so easy."

"Maybe your purchasing choices are a bit restricted these days." As soon as the words were out Janice regretted that comment.

"That's a bit below the belt, Jan."

"I'm sorry."

"I lost my faith a long time ago. I thought I might find it again while I was banged up with only myself for company. But I soon realised if I was to find God he, she or it would be my own creation. It would come from within and that would immediately invalidate the concept."

"My God has always been inside me as well as existing on the outside. A personal God but also the same God I recognise in communal prayer. I've got both a subjective and objective relationship with God." said Janice. "I've always turned to God in both good and bad times."

"Regard yourself as fortunate, I wish it was that easy for me." Janice detected a hint of some of the old cockiness in his voice.

They went 'Dutch' on the bill and left. The drive to Janice's Houghton residence was a good half hour from the restaurant. Justin had inserted an eight-track tape of a Paul Simon album and there was no need for any conversation. After a while the car turned into the Levy's long driveway. Justin stopped near the front door and switched off the engine.

"One of the biggest regrets of my life, and boy there are many," began Justin looking straight ahead. "Yes one of the biggest regrets is letting you go."

"I'm not sure it was a case of you letting me go," said Janice. "We both decided to go our own ways."

"I'm sorry I could have phrased that better. When you left for Israel, I thought ..... I realised-"

"All you were thinking of was yourself and the ANC. I didn't feature at all."

"Yes and it was too late when I realised the mistake I had made. Once you were gone I regretted losing you. I still do. My feelings for you are still the same."

"Well it's all too late now Jus. I've moved on. Too much has happened in the last three years."

"You know you said I should consider going to Israel. What if I did?" Justin turned to look at her and placed a hand on her shoulder.

"I was thinking of *you*. I'm concerned about the state your life is in. That's all."

"That's all?"

"Yes that's all."

Justin moved his hand to stroke the back of her head. Janice began to open the car door.

"Don't go just yet, Jan. "

She hesitated and closed the door again. "Look Justin," she said, "there's nothing to resuscitate here. Our relationship is history."

Justin withdrew his hand. "Why, have you got someone else?"

"Yes. We live together and we've got plans. That doesn't mean you and I can't be friends."

"Sorry. I shouldn't have -"

"It's okay. No problem. I'm sorry I didn't make it clear. I'd better go now. Thank you for a lovely evening." She kissed him on the cheek and left.

Justin started the engine and watched her wave before entering the house.

***

Justin woke and lay in his bed awhile, reflecting on the dream which lingered fresh in his mind. He was playing in the park closely attended by his nanny. Next she was pushing him on the swing. Back and forth he swung, his nanny helping to maintain the momentum. As he swung forward his nanny's face came into focus. It was Janice's face. A black face. Then she swept him off the swing and he was a little boy in her arms. She buried her face in his neck. She began to kiss him, thrusting her tongue deep into his mouth. A crowd had gathered around them chanting, "Janice! Janice!" Then Janice pulled away laughing; now a white Janice. She was laughing, at first gently then hysterically. Suddenly she was gone and he was surrounded by a silent crowd of onlookers, staring sombrely.

Justin lay in bed for a few minutes. He looked across at the empty bed where his roommate had been. The clock on the wall, five minutes fast, read seven thirty. He wasted no time in dressing. Picking up his rucksack, he left the house without checking to see if any of the residents were still there. He was hungry but it didn't matter.

He drove aimlessly for an hour or so until his surroundings had become more rural. When he was satisfied enough signs of civilization had diminished, he found a layby and slinging his rucksack onto his back he walked across the open fields heading for a clump of trees, a kilometre or so in the distance. An isolated farmstead broke the skyline to his left.

Justin strode purposefully across the rough, stubbled terrain. The field wore the charred remains of a successful harvest, ready to face the harshness of winter. Soon he approached the trees and having selected one in a secluded spot in the heart of the group, he removed his rucksack. Placing it on the ground beside him, he sat down, leaning back against the trunk. He sat still for a while. His breathing was calm and controlled. He fixed his gaze on the bark of a tree opposite.

It was a beautiful, clear and fresh morning; a typical Transvaal late autumn morning. The farmer on the distant farmstead had been out feeding his poultry. He looked up to see a flock of birds suddenly rise from the trees a few kilometres in the distance and, regathering themselves, fly off until they were out of sight.

***

Breakfast on Janice's final morning was a quiet affair with much introspection among the three participants. Martin tried his best to read the paper in an attempt to take his mind off his daughter's impending departure. Both Rina and Janice remained quiet preferring to concentrate on eating. Rina had dreaded the arrival of the day. The realisation that her daughter had made a home for herself in Israel had accentuated the gloom which pervaded the Levy household. Henceforth communication would be by letter or the occasional phone call. Rina knew that she and Martin would have to make trips to Israel on a regular, if not annual basis for the foreseeable future.

She was faced with a set of circumstances at odds with motherhood. As a mother she should have an ear and eye on the daily affairs of her daughter. Other mothers within her circle of friends knew what their daughters were up to. They saw them regularly and shared personal information as and when appropriate. She was missing out on so much and consequently was imbued with a deep sense of frustration at the geographical distance which had marked the past three years and which was destined to become a fait accompli in the future.

And so, breakfast on Janice's last morning in South Africa was a subdued affair. A penetrating silence prevailed in the room. It was a remarkably wasteful silence given the circumstances. A cluster of strelizias was framed by the window which looked out onto the garden. Janice had always known the flower as the 'bird of paradise'. Its bright orange 'crest' and deep green 'beak' contrasted splendidly with the rich green of its leaves. Janice studied its detail as a welcome distraction from the somberness of the breakfast table. It reminded her of a hoopoe which had appeared on her small patch of lawn one morning. She had watched it cover every square centimetre of ground as it pecked and probed for food. Then it had floated gently onto the rockery in the corner where it displayed its magnificent crest, filling her with a sense of wonder and well-being. She had felt honoured by its presence; a visitor in her own little patch of Ramat Aviv.

Her thoughts were interrupted by the sound of the telephone ringing. Rina went to answer it and returned within a couple of minutes with a look on her face which Janice understood immediately. She had seen that look several times over the years. She recognised it as the look on her mother's face when her grandmother had passed away; when her school friend Rosanna Leibowitz had been killed by a hit and run driver; when Uncle Abe, her mother's brother, had drowned while on holiday in Plettenberg Bay.

"It's Moira, Jan. Before you go to the phone, I should warn you, it's bad news."

"Bad news? What do you mean?"

"It's Justin. He's shot himself."

"My God! Shot himself!"

"Go to Moira, Jan."

Janice went through to the entrance hall. She herself was in a state of shock. She could feel her heart pounding against her chest as she walked. She put the receiver to her ear.

"Oh Moira! Moira darling, I'm so sorry. I was with him last night."

"Jan .... sorry .... I can't ... I can't speak."

"I wish I could come over Moira. I'm so sorry, I'm flying in three hours."

"I know Jan. I'll write to you. It'll be easier ... easier to gather my thoughts and express myself."

"You take care Moira darling. Love to your parents. I wish you all long life."

"Thanks Jan. You look after yourself."

Janice returned to the dining room desperately trying to control the tears that refused to be held back.

Rina went over to her and held her tightly. Then the tears began to come freely.

1997

Janice Barlev had a deep sense of foreboding as she felt the plane dip conspicuously in readiness for landing. She was ensconced in the middle section of the aircraft and, for most of the flight, had either dozed or shown a vague interest in the images on the screen before her. That her mother was dying was beyond doubt. That she would make it in time to bid her goodbye was far from certain.

When she had received the call to come before it was too late, Janice had managed to arrange her flight within half an hour. Loose ends had been tied up at work at Tel Aviv University before the end of the same afternoon. Her good friend and neighbour, Talia Kahane, was to look after the children while her husband Yossi drove her to Tel Aviv airport to catch that evening's El Al flight to Johannesburg. Yossi himself, a doctor at the local hospital in Tel Aviv, had managed to change his shift to accommodate the sudden turn of events.

She reflected on the haste with which it had all been sorted and the disorientation she had felt as her life had been turned upside down within an hour. She had known about the inevitability of a trip back home, only she had thought it would be later rather than sooner and that more time would have been available to prepare herself mentally and emotionally for her final meeting with her mother.

Rina's cancer had gradually and stubbornly escaped the best efforts of the team of doctors who had spent a good part of eighteen months trying to retrieve a few more years of her life. The last time Janice had seen her mother was when she and Martin had visited Israel five years before, on the occasion of the birth of their fourth grandchild. Rina had been in rude health, having just turned seventy. They had both previously flown out for Janice's wedding which had taken place in Jerusalem in 1986.

This was Janice's first return visit to South Africa since 1977. A new South Africa, an apartheid-free South Africa. A new ANC-led South Africa, with Mandela as president, awaited her arrival at Johannesburg airport, no longer named after former Prime Minister, Jan Smuts. She ought to be feeling excited as all she had hoped and prayed for had come to pass. She was about to land in a free, democratic, multi-racial country, no longer the pariah of the world. Yet her life had changed over the years. She was now an Israeli citizen married to an Israeli man with two Israeli children who had never set foot in the land of her birth. She had retained a strong interest in South Africa's affairs but no longer had the same passion she had felt all those years ago as a young woman imbued with political fervour and an all-consuming sense of justice.

She no longer felt the same sense of identity with the change movement. The transformation of the political landscape had occurred *in spite of* her. There had been no cause and effect as far as she was concerned. She realised there and then, as she was about to land, that she was not in fact coming 'home'. She was travelling on an Israeli passport. She mostly thought in Hebrew these days. Although she had ensured that her children were reasonably fluent in English, the language spoken at home was Hebrew. She was a foreigner about to land in the country of her birth.

Her thoughts turned to her mother. During her formative adult years, a gulf had opened up between them. Janice's involvement in politics had ensured mother and daughter seldom agreed. Now that Janice was a mature woman with children of her own, a new bond had been established and she had enjoyed the time they had spent together when Rina and Martin had visited in 1992. The focus of that visit was to meet six-month-old Ari, their grandson. Janice and her mother had been preoccupied with domestic matters and, apart from Mandela's release from prison, politics had never featured as a topic for discussion. Janice felt sad that her mother had never met her granddaughter Tziporah. Barring a miracle that meeting would never take place.

Martin and Jonathan were standing at the exit waiting for her. She knew immediately that her mother had died. They approached her grim-faced and before she could greet him, Martin had buried his face in her shoulder sobbing quietly. She embraced him for a few seconds cupping the back of his head in a maternal gesture.

Then Martin drew back and whispered, "She's gone darling."

Janice remained silent and allowed the tears that had already filled her eyes to run freely down her cheeks. She looked across at Jonathan who taken charge of her luggage trolley. He smiled weakly. It had been such a long time, something like twenty years since they had seen each other. In that time he had grown a beard, prematurely flecked with grey. He was clearly following in the footsteps of other Levy men who had lost the struggle to retain a full head of hair.

Although she had seen photographs of Jonathan during the years they had been apart, she was nevertheless somewhat taken aback to see this much changed man who was clearly her brother in several respects but a perfect stranger in others.

Jonathan hugged her warmly. Neither spoke, in mutual acknowledgement that the occasion required silence.

***

Twenty years on had seen a transformation in the Levy milieu that Janice re-entered. Both Joseph and Mary had left. Apparently Mary had returned to KwaZulu Natal. Joseph had passed away six years before with a liver complaint directly linked to his inordinate drinking problem. A spate of unsuccessful employees had been tried until finally stability had been achieved in recent months in the form of a middle-aged woman Gertie and a young man Gabriel.

The house was still much the same with some minor changes having been made to the furnishings. Janice immediately noticed a new lounge suite and all the curtains were different. Every mirror in the house, apart from those in bathrooms, was covered. Janice found the custom disconcerting. It added to the sense of gloom. She was not one for communal customs and traditions. She preferred to respond to occurrences and events as an individual. If there were to be any traditions to be followed they ought to be family traditions.

"What will you do, Daddy?" asked Janice, when they were at the dining room table that evening.

"I've decided to sell up and find a small town house somewhere. There are several new housing complexes in Jo'burg. Condos I think they're called."

"I'm pleased to hear that. I can't stand the thought of you on your own in this house. Apart from the upkeep it'll accentuate your loneliness. You're making the right decision." Janice leaned across the table and held her father's hand. "What does Jonnie think? Does he think you're doing the right thing?"

"Yes he agrees there's no point in staying here. Too many memories." Martin squeezed his daughter's hand. His eyes welled up and Janice stood and went to give him a hug. Martin sat with his elbows on the table, face in hands and released the tears he had been fighting back for a while. Janice bent over her father and held him tightly.

"I'm looking forward to you meeting your sister-in-law and nephews," said Martin after composing himself.

"I've spoken to Paula briefly on the phone so it will be good to finally get to know her. The last time I was here Jonathan was trying to persuade you and mom to accept his girl-friend Helen."

"Really! It was that long ago you were home last." Martin squeezed her hand.

"Is Jonnie happy Dad? I've had very little contact with him so I haven't been able to gauge how things are. I gather she and mum didn't really hit off."

"They tolerated each other to a large extent. Your mother thought she had some strange ideas about bringing up children."

"Anyway Dad I'm exhausted. You just be tired too. I'm going to bed if that's okay. Is there anything you want me to do before I go to bed?"

"We could both do with a good night's sleep darling. We've got a difficult day tomorrow. Good night darling."

***

Jonathan's voice quivered on the icy winter breeze:

"Yitgadal v'yitkadash sh'mei rabbah".

He drew a deep breath in anticipation of the congregation's *"Amein"*. Delving into the depths of his inner resources he continued:

"B'alimah dee v'rah chir'utei v'yamlich malchutei. B'chayeichon, uv'yomeichon, uv'chayei d'chol beit yisroel, ba'agalah u'vizman kariv v'imru:" The congregation came in again with

"Amein."

Jonathan suddenly became aware of his shivering body. He composed himself as the congregation took over.

"Y'hei sh'mei rabbah m'vorach l'allam u'l'allmei allmayah."

He drew comfort from their intervention. He no longer felt alone and exposed. It had become a joint, communal effort now and he continued, gaining confidence all the while:

"Yitborach, v'yishtabach, v'yitpo'ar, viyitromam, viyitnassei, v'yit'hador, v'yit'aleh, v'yit'hallal ....".

Jonathan's voice floated away as Janice relaxed slightly, turning inwards to her own thoughts. Yet she maintained a firm hold on Martin's arm. His body was

101

trembling from a combination of the cold breeze and the situation. She thought about the incongruous maleness of the scene. The congregation's deep-throated male drone. The dark suits which dominated the hundred or so congregants. The rabbi and cantor, both in black with long grey beards. Then she imagined her mother's body, petite and ultimately frail, laid out inside the coffin.

Janice closed her eyes and tried to remember the last time she had seen her alive. She managed to evoke the scene at Tel Aviv airport. Her mother had turned at the entrance to the "Passengers Only" area. She had given one last wave and the trademark blown kiss, all the while clinging to her husband for support. The trip had been a mother-daughter bonding experience. Janice had been surprised at the ease with which she and Rina had allowed their thoughts and opinions to dovetail. The common, dominant experience of motherhood had ensured there was much to talk about. Janice's maturation into motherhood had meant she was preoccupied with doing her best for her two young children. The fire that had once burned within her young belly had become the warm glow of motherhood.

Her thoughts were interrupted by signs of movement around her. Martin had released himself from her hold and was walking towards the open grave. He picked up the spade which had been left beside it and gently cast three spadefuls of soil onto his wife's coffin. He stood and stared down into the grave for a few seconds before handing the spade to Jonathan who repeated the ritual. In turn all the men followed suit.

Janice went over to give her brother a hug. "Well done Jonnie," she whispered. "We're proud of you."

Her brother clung to her. He tried to say' Thank you," but the words wouldn't come out. He had dreaded the day and now the worst was over. After a while he pulled away. Janice gave him a tissue.

Paula had stayed in the background throughout. She had always been quite peripheral in family affairs since marrying Jonathan and she preferred to let her husband depend on Martin and Janice for any support he might need.

The family stood at the cemetery exit to receive the congregants as they made their way out. Janice had been away so long she recognised only a small minority of those who shook her hand or kissed her as they filed past. Finally the rabbi, recently arrived from the United States, approached the family. Martin thanked him for officiating so sympathetically. Janice wondered how well he had known her mother. At least he had done his research and managed to load his eulogy with some credible, recognisable virtues her mother had been known to possess. The most regrettable aspect of the service for Janice had been its inflexibility, which, apart from Jonathan's de rigueur Kaddish item, didn't allow for input from the family.

Janice had largely turned her back on religion and apart from the occasional wedding or funeral there had been little reason to confront the rituals of Judaism in either its most extreme or more watered down form as proselytised by the Reform movement. Her son had been circumcised at the behest of Yossi who still adhered to much of his religious upbringing. Living in Israel meant that you were always aware of the influence of the religiosity of the environment. Indeed, it was impossible to ignore the different atmosphere of Friday nights and Saturdays, although Tel Aviv had a more secular atmosphere than Jerusalem. Generally speaking, an acceptable balance between secularity and religion prevailed in the Barlev household. Janice was not as such a lapsed Jew, but neither did she allow religion to control her daily life.

So, when the rabbi came to her house that night for prayers, Janice did not take kindly to being required to sit on a low bench while greeting friends and members of the extended family as they arrived. She wondered why their misery had to be on show. She wanted to mourn privately, enveloped in her own thoughts and memories away from others. By the end of the first night of seven nights of prayers she had had enough. She wanted to escape and the Janice of twenty years ago would have done so. The more mature Janice realised her father needed support.

Later that evening the immediate family gathered at Jonathan's house for dinner. The four-bedroom house was situated in Sandton, in the north of the city of Johannesburg. Jonathan, his wife Paula and their two sons, David and Sam, age six and eight respectively, had lived there for the past five years.

Janice had only just met Paula and the boys for the first time and was taking a while to warm to them. Paula had remained discreetly in the background ever since her arrival and the boys had continued to attend school, so there had been little contact until now. They had been considered too young to attend the funeral although Jonathan had made a strong case to the contrary.

"I think they will both be able to cope," he had asserted, but Paula was adamant they should be spared the ordeal.

"I don't see the point in exposing them to the trauma at such an early age," she had said. "Let them remember your mother without having to see her being lowered into the ground. There's no reason why they shouldn't attend school; it'll take their minds off it."

Paula Abrahams and Jonathan had been married for ten years. They had met at a party in Cape Town while Jonathan was on holiday. After a year-long courtship, mostly by proxy, Jonathan had persuaded her to move up to Johannesburg where they rented a small flat for a while before deciding to get married. Rina had referred to Paula as a "cold fish" and the relationship between the two women was often strained. Although she conceded that Paula was a good example of a balabusta, she had detected a steady diminishing of Jonathan's spirit in recent years. He had slotted too easily into his role as provider, while Paula had become family manager, making all the major decisions to most of which Jonathan somewhat graciously and often meekly acquiesced.

After dinner that evening Martin offered to teach Sam chess. It provided a useful focal point for the rest of the family who sat and watched.

"Mom would have been so pleased to see Dad and Sam playing together," said Jonathan.

"I'm sure she's looking down right now, enjoying the sigh-," said Martin, the sudden lump in his throat thwarting the end of the sentence.

Standing behind him, Janice put her arms around her father and kissed him lightly on the top of his head. Trying to lift the sudden gloom that had filled the room, she chuckled, "I felt a bit of bare skin then, you'll need to start wearing a kippah permanently if you lose any more hair."

"That's mean," said Jonathan. "He's doing alright for sixty-eight. He's till playing golf twice a week."

"You can't move there Sam my boy. Remember your knight moves in an 'L' shape. Either two forward or back and then one sideways or vice versa."

"What's vice versa, Grandpa?"

"It just means the other way, a bit like the opposite."

Martin demonstrated the various moves of a knight and the game continued until he decided it was time to explain check mate.

"Can you see why I've got your king trapped? Look it can't move anywhere. Wherever it goes it will be in check. Can you see that?"

Janice winked at Jonathan. Their father was back in his element. He loved playing games and chess was his favourite.

A short while later the boys were sent upstairs to bed. Janice volunteered to read them a story. She felt the need to try to forge a bond with her nephews.

"Have you got a favourite story?" asked Janice

"Not really," said Sam. "We don't normally have stories at night."

"Maybe we can go to a bookshop tomorrow. I would love to buy you each a book."

"Thanks Aunty Janice."

"Okay for now I will tell you the story of Purim. Once there was a King named Ahasuerus whose wife

Vashti refused to obey his command to parade herself in front of the people. He decided to replace her with a new queen chosen from the most beautiful young women in the land. Amongst these was a Jewish girl named Esther-"

"Do you think Vashti was right to refuse Aunty Jan?" asked David. "Would you have refused?"

"Things were different in those days," said Janice. "A king was the ruler of the land. Nowadays we have a president in charge and the president is chosen by the people and can be removed by the people. It's called democracy."

"Our president is Nelson Mandela," said Sam.

"Indeed he is," declared Janice, a hint of pride in her voice. "Maybe tomorrow night I will tell you the story of our president who went from prison to become leader of our nation."

"Why do you say 'our president' Aunty Jan, when you live in Israel?" asked Sam.

"That's a good question, Sam. A very good question. Just because you live somewhere else it doesn't mean you forget your past. I used to live here. One day I hope you two will visit me in Israel and you can meet your cousins."

When Janice finished the story of Purim she kissed the boys and turned off the light. She met Paula on the staircase.

"All okay?" asked Paula.

"All quiet," said Janice.

"I'm off to bed," said Paula." I've got a bit of a headache."

"Oh. Sorry to hear that. Hope you're feeling better in the morning."

"Thanks. See you tomorrow. Good night."

"Good night, Paula." Janice hovered on the staircase for a few moments. What was it about her sister-in-law that made her feel uneasy? There was a definite coldness about her demeanour which unsettled Janice.

Downstairs Martin and Jonathan were having a nightcap in the lounge. "Alright Jan? All quiet in the dormitory?"

"All quiet. Sorry Paula's not well."

"Ah she's got one of her headaches. Not unusual."

"Am I interrupting something?" asked Janice.

"Not at all. We could do with your contribution. Dad and I were discussing what happens next."

Martin stood up and walked over to the drinks cabinet to top up his whisky. "Another?" he indicated to Jonathan. "What about you darling? Will you join us?"

"No thanks Dad, I've got to drive you home don't forget. So what were you discussing?"

Martin topped up his whisky and took the bottle over to Jonathan. "We were talking about what I should do with my life next. I'm going to move as soon as possible but Jonnie thinks I should stay here ... with him ... until I find something."

Janice immediately visualised Paula's face at hearing her father-in-law was going to move in, even for a relatively brief period. "Dad what about having an extended holiday in Israel? You could come back with me for a couple of months."

Martin chuckled, almost dismissively. He sat down and sipped his whisky. "That would be lovely but I can't just leave everything. There's too much to do here."

"That's nonsense," said Jonathan. "I can sort everything out. Give me power of attorney and I can see to all the loose ends. It'll do you good. You can spend time with your other grandchildren and at the same time clear your head in readiness for the future. We could put the house on the market and even start storing stuff. You need a break from all this -"

"All what? What's *all this*?" said Martin.

"Look you've been through hell for a few months now," continued Jonathan. "You're in mourning and you could do with some time in a different environment. And where better than Israel?"

Janice was grateful for Jonathan's support. She dreaded leaving her father again, especially under the circumstances. It would be a traumatic experience for both. Each farewell was worse than the last. Spending two months or so with her in Israel would be the ideal solution all round. The prospect of her father ensnared by his aloneness in his large house at night would make it difficult for her to return to Israel with peace of mind.

Martin's silence was a promising sign. At least he was contemplating the suggestion.

"Remind me when you're going back," said Jonathan.

"I'm leaving next Tuesday morning, but if necessary I can change the ticket. If you want to come with me, Dad and you need more time, I could stay a few more days."

"Let me think about things overnight," said Martin. "It's all a bit sudden and I need to be sure it's the right thing to do."

***

Martin joined his daughter at the breakfast table. Janice was engrossed in the The Star, poring over an article about Mandela's first three years as president. So far so good was the main thrust of the article. The honeymoon period was still going strong and the whites had taken their new president to their collective bosom. Madiba. Our Madiba. The writer of the article was a Jakobus van Rensburg who was on the staff of Die Beeld. Writing for The Star he was aware of the kind of audience he had. The educated whites of leafy Johannesburg suburbia were being stroked gently as van Rensburg analysed how the rainbow nation was being drawn into the circle of the civilised West. Indeed they had hosted and memorably won the rugby World Cup. It had been a signal that this reinvigorated, vibrant country was no longer *'natio non grata'*. The doubters among the white community had had their spirits lifted, albeit temporarily. Mandela's donning of a Springbok jersey had signaled his intent to be an inclusive president.

"Morning darling."

"Morning. I'm just catching up on Mandela's first three years in office," said Janice. "You okay. Sleep well?"

"Not too bad, " said Martin. "It's still strange waking up to a half empty bed. Whose article is that?"

"It's an Afrikaans journalist from Die Beeld. Generally quite positive. It seems the honeymoon is continuing and is likely to until the next election. Presumably he won't continue after that – surely he'll be too old. If I were him I would opt for the quite life at the age of eighty or so."

Martin sat down opposite her and began to pour his cereal into the bowl before him. "Nothing much is different these days. The so-called petty apartheid has mostly gone. The black middle class is evident in the suburbs now. But unemployment is still high and there is still a lot of poverty in the townships. We whites, by and large, keep our heads down and get on with our lives."

"Is that not a bit dangerous? Will the black electorate not become impatient?" Janice passed him the milk.

"I'm sure they will. I think Mandela is fortunate in many ways. Because of his age he is likely to have only one term. Whoever comes after him will have to pick up the tab. Mandela's status as a living legend in the eyes of the world will remain intact."

"I suppose the biggest threat will be a brain drain. If white professionals start leaving there won't be enough time to fill the gaps with equally well-educated blacks. Anyway I still find it all very exciting coming back to so many changes. Have you thought any more about my suggestion?"

"I will come Jan, but not right now. I need to sort things out in the next month or so and then I will come over to you."

"I wish I could stay longer but I should get back. Jonnie has offered-"

"I need time to sort things *myself.* I want to put this house on the market. I can't just leave everything now.

I wouldn't relax in Israel knowing there's so much to do. I promise I will come over soon and I do appreciate your offer. I just wouldn't feel comfortable leaving so many loose ends."

"What are you doing today?" asked Janice. "I wouldn't mind buying some clothes and some other bits for the kids. Do you want to come with me to Sandton City?"

"I think I'll stay put and begin sorting myself out. You take Mom's car. It needs a run."

Janice stood up and went over to her father on the opposite side of the table. She gave him a hug from behind. "Okay, thanks Dad. Let me know if you need anything. I'll leave in about an hour."

***

The Sandton traffic was particularly heavy that morning and it was a while before Janice joined the queue to enter the car park. Once through the barrier she managed to find a parking spot on the ground floor reasonably close to the entrance to the shops. Once inside she hardly recognised the place. There was a vibrant buzz as shoppers, many of whom were black, filled the concourse. There was much evidence that a strong black middle class had begun to emerge in the new South Africa.

An hour or so later Janice returned to the car park laden with the fruits of her shopping expedition. She loaded her car boot with the various shopping bags and went to the ticket machine to pay for her parking. As always the cost of the parking was a pleasant surprise and she returned to the car, unaware that a figure had emerged from between two of the vehicles parked near hers.

The next few seconds were to be indelibly impressed on her memory. Just as she was opening the door of her mother's car, the parking ticket and car keys were snatched from her grasp and she was pushed to the ground banging her head on the wheel of the car in the next bay. As she lay on the ground she saw a large dark figure scramble into the driver's seat. Janice tried to scream but only the faintest whimper emerged from her mouth. She felt a sharp pain at the back of her head as she tried to sit up. She heard the engine start and the car reversed, followed by a screeching of tyres as it sped out of sight.

Slowly she levered herself to a sitting position, resting her back against the car door. She felt the back of her head; warm blood trickled through her fingers from a large gash caused by the rim of the car's wheel. The pain was now accompanied by a throbbing within her head. An overpowering stench of fumes and oil filled her nostrils. Everything around her was turning. She was a little girl again on a funfair ride as she felt herself gyrate violently. Soon she was drifting, floating. Like a leaf in the wind she was swirling gently into the blue sky.

***

Janice opened her eyes. A pair of bright fluorescent lights on the white ceiling made her blink. She was aware of a pain at the back of her head and tried to turn over onto her side. However the pain in her hip forced her to remain on her back. Her surroundings were suddenly recognisable. She was in hospital. How and why were not so clear and she struggled to assemble her thoughts and make sense of her situation.

She remembered walking back to the car park with her shopping bags, but nothing else. She knew she had been shopping and had bought some clothes for her return to Israel. A piece of her life had apparently disappeared, for here she was lying in a hospital bed and in some pain if she dared to move.

"She's awake!" Janice recognised her brother's voice. "Welcome to the new South Africa!" said Jonathan. "You should have been warned."

"Hello Jonnie," mewled Janice. "Hello Dad. What happ-"

"Take it easy darling," said Martin. "We'll talk about it later. How are you feeling?"

"I've felt better," said Janice, her voice struggling to regain a degree of resonance. "My head hurts. S-something's happened to my hip; it's bloody sore if I move. Ouch!" Janice tried to turn her body to face the door of her private ward.

"Take it easy," said Martin. "Just relax. You've been in the wars." He bent over and kissed her on the cheek. A bandage was wrapped around her head, just above her eyebrows.

"Jonnie, what happened? What do you mean I should've been warned?"

"Can't you remember? " Jonathan went round to the opposite side of the bed and gently took her hand.

"No. I know I went shopping ... I remember going back to the car park and paying at the machine ... after that there's a blank."

"Jan why do you think you're in pain?" asked Jonathan squeezing her hand gently.

"I..I must have fallen I suppose. I feel as though I've banged my head on something."

Jonathan cast an enquiring look in Martin's direction.

"Jan darling," said Martin. "You were knocked to the ground. Some... someone took mom's car."

Janice closed her eyes. She didn't respond for a few moments. When she opened them again Martin and Jonathan were whispering in the corner of the room.

"You mean I was carjacked!"

Martin approached the bed again. "Yes darling. You were carjacked."

"I was lucky. I'm lucky to be lying here, aren't I?"

"I wouldn't say that. I suppose it ... it could've been worse," said Martin.

"And the car? Mom's car? Have they found it?"

"Not yet."

"I don't think we'll see Mom's car again," said Jonathan. " They'll have sold it by now. It's probably in another part of the country already. It happens every day now. The police can't cope any longer."

Janice tried to sit up, wincing as she manoeuvred her body into a sitting position. Martin gently supported her while rearranging her pillows to make her more comfortable.

"Thanks Dad. I should've been more careful. I was holding both the keys and the parking ticket."

"That's the way things are here now," said Jonathan. "Jo'burg is the new crime capital of the

115

world. It's so common it doesn't make the newspapers any more."

"Have you contacted Yossi and the kids?" asked Janice.

"He wanted to fly over immediately. I told him to wait until we'd seen you," said Martin.

"There's no point," said Janice. "I'm okay thank goodness. It's going to take time before things settle down There was always going to be some upheaval as people were free to move around."

"People are pouring into the cities and they can't cope. There's no planning. Not enough jobs, not enough accommodation."

A nurse, a black woman of about thirty, walked in at that moment. "Excuse me gentlemen. How are you feeling Mrs Barlev? Any pain?"

"Not too bad thanks nurse. My head is throbbing a bit."

"I'll bring you a painkiller. Can I get you anything else? Tea maybe?"

"That would be great," said Janice. "Thanks."

"I'll be back soon. Can I get you some tea as well?" said the nurse looking at Martin and Jonathan.

"Thank you," said Jonathan.

"Yes please, I would love a cup of tea," said Martin. The nurse smiled and left the room.

"She's from Zimbabwe," said Jonathan. "I think the hospital recruited her as there is a severe shortage. Another sign of the new South Africa. You wouldn't have had a black nurse looking after you a few years ago."

"And how fantastic is that!" said Janice, her voice showing signs of increased animation. "No more petty apartheid!"

"They are going to have to train up some nurses pretty quickly, not to mention doctors and other specialist jobs in health," said Jonathan. "There's a skills shortage in this country which means there's a disaster waiting to happen."

"As long as the local blacks don't start resenting the skilled immigrants in the meantime," said Martin, anxiously looking at his watch. "I need to go Jonnie, I've got an appointment with my lawyer in half an hour. Will you excuse us Jan? I'll be back later tonight. Visiting hours are from seven so I'll see you then."

"Bye Jan. See you when you're out of here. I'm sure it won't be more than a couple of days." Jonathan kissed his sister on the cheek and the two men left the room.

Janice lay on her back for a while desperately trying to recall the incident that filled the gap between her entering the car park and ending up in her present state in a hospital bed. To an extent she was relieved that the undoubted trauma of the incident had not left its mark on her memory, but she was also filled with deep disappointment that something so violent had happened to her, of all people. She had tried her best to embrace and understand the change that had taken place in her country since she had left so many years ago. She had been excited by the visible, albeit relatively superficial transformation which had been evident from the time she had arrived at Johannesburg airport. And yet the old feelings had come rushing back as she had engaged with the people within the 'whiteness' of her social milieu. Many of their comments, albeit made with a faux sheepishness and a touch of recently developed self-consciousness, retained undertones of racism. A new sector of the population appeared to have emerged, mostly referred to as 'they'. 'They' do this or 'they' do that. The changes since Mandela's release were viewed from a discreet distance as if politics were a sort of spectator sport for whites. The city centre had become a refuge for migrant blacks from the old bantustans and the whites had seen fit to escape to the suburbs, often building barricades around themselves. The thriving security industry was evident everywhere. Her family home had been turned into a fortress.

Even the term 'rainbow nation', which connoted beauty and hope, implied an obsession with colour which was unlikely to disappear for years to come. There was the increasing prospect of quotas whether in the allocation of university places or the selection of the nation's rugby team.

And now Janice had experienced first-hand what she had heard about so often in recent times. She was desperate to retain a sense of perspective and not allow this travesty to blur her perception of what had occurred since the end of apartheid. Even so she was filled with a deep sense of foreboding and despair. What had she expected? The romanticism of the struggle and the hopes that came with that were evaporating fast as South Africa found its feet in the world of nations. It was an emerging, vibrant democracy doing its best to disengorge itself of the excesses of the apartheid era. White South Africa had feasted on the fruits of black labour for decades and the process of change was bound to be difficult, if not painful, as the new nation found its place in the real world.

The incident made her feel even more isolated and foreign. She missed her husband and children and was experiencing a feeling that could only be described as homesickness.

Soon, she fell into an uneasy sleep.

***

When Janice opened her eyes again later that afternoon, the face of her sister-in-law came slowly into focus. Her head was still throbbing and the pain in her back caused her to wince as she tried to prop herself up.

"Paula! Nice to see you!"

"Hello Janice. How are you?" Paula was standing at the door and approached the bed. "Can I help you?"

"Thanks. Can you just move these pillows so I can sit up more?" said Janice. "Good of you to come."

"There. How does that feel?" asked Paula in the matter-of-fact manner of a nurse. She sat down on the chair beside Janice's bed.

"Fine thank you. Where are the boys?"

"They're at home with the maid. I didn't think they should come this time. It sounds as though you've had a nasty experience."

"Thankfully I can't remember a thing. I'm just feeling the after-effects."

"That's how we live here," said Paula. "The new, improved South Africa isn't the paradise some thought it would be. You never know what's around the corner. You watch your back; you lock car doors."

Janice took advantage of the need to shift herself into a more comfortable position in order to avoid having to respond. She was deeply disappointed that it had come to this. However, she was determined not to allow all the hope and promise to be extinguished by this one event.

"Jonathan and I haven't ruled out the possibility of emigrating," continued Paula. "My father was born in London and I've held a British passport since I left school."

"Have you ever been to the UK?" asked Janice.

"No, but we're happy to give it a go. I'm sure we'd slot in quite happily."

"What does Jonathan think?"

"He's obviously worried about leaving your father. He thinks he's at an age now when he wouldn't be able to cope on his own for too long."

The throbbing in Janice's head was beginning to trouble her. "Well he's just lost his life-long partner so he's vulnerable at the moment. Can you bear with me for a minute? I just want to call for a nurse. I need to take a painkiller."

Paula stood up and went to the door. "I'll see if I can get one. Hold on a minute."

Janice wasn't sure about Paula. Reading between the lines of her mother's letters she had formed an image of someone who found it difficult to reach out and embrace family life. She remembered her mother's reference to her as a "cold fish". Since her arrival in Johannesburg Janice was yet to hold a conversation with Paula who seemed content to remain outside of the family loop in its period of mourning. She sensed that this hospital visit might prove a welcome opportunity to begin to form a relationship with her sister-in-law.

Paula came back accompanied by the nurse from Zimbabwe, who gave Janice something to relieve her headache.

"Thanks Paula," said Janice. "It shouldn't take too long to have an effect. It seems I banged my head on the wheel of a car."

Paula resumed her seat. "You know I said your dad wouldn't be able to cope on his own," she began. "Well it seems Jonathan is keen for him to come and live with us."

"Yes he did mention it to me."

"On the face of it it's a logical step," continued Paula in the same matter-of-fact tone which seemed to characterise her social intercourse in general. "However I'm not sure it *is* such a good idea. Three generations in one household doesn't always work."

The throbbing in Janice's head was making it difficult for her to engage with Paula. Nevertheless, she sensed that this was not intended as an ice-breaking visit after all. It was clear that Paula had a different agenda.

Paula waited for a response from Janice but there was none. "I'm concerned that the relationship between the boys and your dad will be affected," she continued. "I mean they need the space to live their lives as normal, noisy and boisterous children and your dad .. .. well he needs to be able to choose when he would prefer peace and quiet."

Janice couldn't find fault with that point of view. It was just Paula's motives that concerned her. Perhaps she should give her the benefit of the doubt.

"Maybe your house wouldn't be suitable anyway," said Janice helpfully.

"Jonnie is talking about an extension," said Paula. "He thinks it would be an investment. He argues that if it was self-contained, your dad would have his privacy and the boys could be themselves."

Janice's doubts about Paula's motives were strengthening by the second. "What do you think about that idea?" she asked.

"I'm not convinced it would work. There would still be mealtimes and then of course there's the cost. It all seems a bit too long-term, too final. Especially if there's a possibility of us emigrating."

Janice's frustration was increasing and although her headache was less intense she was longing to lie back and rest. She bent forward and reached behind her back to adjust a pillow. Letting out an exaggerated sigh of pain she slowly shifted her body into a flatter position. Reading the sign Paula stood up.

"I'm off now Janice. I'll leave you in peace. I hope you get better soon."

"Thanks Paula. Love to Jonathan and the boys and thanks for coming."

"That's okay. Bye for now." Paula turned and left the room.

Janice closed her eyes. She was relieved that she didn't have to continue what was developing into an awkward conversation. It was clear that Martin's future was going to cause a problem in the Levy household. Even so she was able to see Paula's point of view.

Paula's widowed mother lived in Cape Town independent of her family and why should Paula be asked to incorporate her father-in-law into the mainstream of her life. It was clear that she should pursue the idea of Martin spending a few months with her in Israel and then reassess his situation. The possibility of Jonathan and his family emigrating changed the situation anyway. Much would depend on Martin's ability to manage life as a widower after forty years of marriage. How would he take to growing old on his own with none of his immediate family around him?

"How are you feeling Mrs. Barlev?" asked the nurse. She had entered so quietly that Janice was startled out of her reverie. "I'm so sorry, did I wake you. I saw your visitor leave and I assumed you were awake."

"Not to worry. I was awake – just lying and thinking," said Janice. My headache is much better thank you. I hear you are from Zimbabwe. What brought you here?"

"I heard there was a shortage of nurses so I applied through the SA government. I have family in Johannesburg. Things are not too good in my country. Now that the government has changed in South Africa, I decided to try for a job here."

"I'm sorry to hear about Zimbabwe. It was always a beacon of hope after independence. I had such faith in Mugabe."

"Mugabe has turned into a dictator. Everywhere you go there are photographs of him. That's always a bad sign. He behaves as if the country *belongs* to him rather than being its leader. Anyway, just press that button if you need me for anything. I'll let you rest."

***

The weather had taken a turn for the worse. Martin and Janice were huddled beneath Martin's golf umbrella as they made their way along the path flanked on either side by graves and tombstones of all shapes and sizes. Janice was carrying a large bunch of white roses in one hand while she and her father jointly held the umbrella handle. Eventually they came to a mound of freshly dug earth marked by a small wooden sign bearing the inscription *"Rina Levy"*.

Janice stepped forward into the rain and leaned the bunch of flowers against the mound. Father and daughter stood for a while in silence staring at the grave. Janice clung to her father whose tears were rolling freely down his cheeks. The noise of the rain on the umbrella seemed appropriate for the moment as father and daughter contemplated their loss. It was Martin who decided that it was time to go as he steered his daughter away and they returned slowly to the exit in silence. Martin washed his hands at the exit and removed his yarmulke. Janice accompanied him to the car.

"Would you mind if I stayed a while," asked Janice. "I won't be long."

She left him and returned to the first set of graves near the entrance. She walked amongst the graves until she found the one she was looking for. She read the inscription on the tombstone:

Justin Greenspan
Passed way suddenly 12.6.1977
Deeply mourned by his loving parents and sister.

Janice stood for a couple of minutes. She felt obliged to pay her respects after all those years. The news had disturbed her for a long while after, especially as she had been with him the night before and had let him down so badly. Inevitably she had felt a degree of responsibility, despite the reassurances she had received from her parents and friends she had confided in when she was back in Israel.

"Oh dear Justin," she mused, "you never lived to see everything you strove for come to pass. All that self-absorption, that unwillingness to allow space for relationships. What for I ask? How can your self-sacrifice be measured? They either break you or they kill you, like Biko. We can't all be Mandelas, Tambos, Sisulus. Besides they were inside the struggle – you were a mere white outsider after all. At least they didn't kill you. You had that decision in your own hands. You never gave them that satisfaction."

Standing before Justin's grave she was particularly disturbed by the positioning of his and the handful of other graves marked out for special treatment, owing to the manner of their deaths. Justin's father was buried near other members of the Greenspan family elsewhere in the cemetery.

***

The visit from the police confirmed that Rina's car had been found in a remote field near Roodepoort in the western region of Gauteng. It had been plundered for a variety of parts including its wheels. They had failed thus far to arrest the man responsible for the crime, but assured Martin and Janice they would continue to investigate.

"Absolutely no chance," said Martin once they had left. "You never hear of any car theft being solved."

"Oh well at least they say they are trying. And, of course, I'm nearly fully recovered," said Janice trying to make light of it.

"Are you sure you are fit to fly tomorrow?"

"Yes. Yossi has upgraded me to business class so I won't be too uncomfortable; and my head is much better. I can use a ring cushion behind my head on the plane."

"Anyway darling, all being well I'll join you in a couple of months from now."

"I will only be happy when you've booked and I know the date you'll arrive," said Janice giving her father a hug.

2017

David Levy looked out of the Airbus window to see the coastline below. The plane had begun its descent to Ben Gurion airport. Ben Gurion, a name associated with the beginning of the modern State of Israel. Ben Gurion, a fighter and pioneer. The first Prime Minister. A man of legendary status in the world of modern Jewry. That was what he had been led to believe, growing up within the Jewish social milieu in Hampstead.

During his years at UCL medical school David had travelled his own, somewhat lonely journey through the world of politics. His left wing radical views on a range of issues had flourished within the seedbed of his formative adult years. His membership of the Young Socialists and refusal to embrace his Jewish heritage had been a source of despair and disappointment to his parents and the rest of his family. Moreover, he had been a member of the Jews for a Free Palestine movement for three years and he had offered to self-fund the forthcoming visit and produce a report on the current state of the Palestinian cause.

His decision to see the situation in Israel and the Palestinian occupied territories for himself had come as a surprise, not least to his aunt who was awaiting his arrival at the airport in Tel Aviv. Janice Barlev hadn't seen David or his brother Sam for some twenty years since meeting them on her return to Johannesburg to attend her mother's funeral.

David's visit had the potential to cause friction within her household. Her husband Yossi was a staunch supporter of the Likud government with little tolerance when it came to considering the cause of Palestinians.

Janice's own children had been made welcome in recent years during visits to England and she felt obliged to reciprocate on this occasion. Yet she felt a sense of unease as she waited for his plane to land. She knew her nephew had a reputation for espousing some "extreme" views on the left of the political spectrum. She knew nothing of his plans during this three-week visit. In David's last email to her he had referred to the visit as a "fact-finding mission".

***

"Welcome to Israel!" Janice offered her nephew both cheeks and invited him to follow her to the car park.

David followed dutifully pushing his trolley along the concourse with the insouciance of a seasoned traveller to whom this was yet another arrival at yet another international airport. It was certainly no pilgrimage for this young man who regarded Zionism as one of the world's political iniquities and for whom his upbringing has been more of a hindrance than a guiding light for living his life. Initially he had eschewed the idea of meeting up with his Israeli section of the family, let alone staying with them, until he realised he would never be forgiven and it would create an unnecessary rift with his father.

"So what are your plans?" asked Janice once they were on the road back to the condominium in Ramat Hasharon in the northern part of metropolitan Tel Aviv. After several years in Jerusalem she and Yossi had moved back to Tel Aviv since being headhunted as a consultant by the local hospital. Janice was more than happy to return to the city where she had spent her first very happy years of life in Israel.

"Well if it's okay with you I would like to spend some time in Tel Aviv until the weekend and then I'm off to Jersualem."

"That's absolutely fine. So how long do you intend staying in Jerusalem?"

Jonathan hesitated briefly before answering." I've got some contacts - some friends - in Jerusalem who will be travelling with me for the rest of my time here."

"So will we get to see you again towards the end? Presumably you will be going back from Ben Gurion again."

"Ah I'm not really sure. It's possible I may end up in Jordan towards the end. And possibly even fly back from Amman."

Both fell silent for a brief time as Janice tried to negotiate her way out of the airport area. Once they were back on the main road to Tel Aviv she resumed her questioning. "Apart from Jerusalem where else will you be going? No doubt there are the usual sites: Dead Sea and Masada; maybe even Galilee?"

"Not too sure really," said David. "A lot depends on what will be organised for me. I do need to visit the West Bank at some stage and also Gaza."

Janice didn't respond. It was a good few minutes before she broke the silence. "Of course you do realise the risks involved. Do your parents know about your plans?"

"I've got some good Palestinian contacts who will look after me. This trip is being facilitated by an organisation I belong to. It's not really a holiday."

"Young, bold and adventurous eh? Some would say foolhardy and even stupid. Look I don't want to patronise you but do you fully understand what you are doing? This is not Europe. We are at war here."

"I need to do this Aunty Janice. I need to understand things from both sides. I can't accept there is only one side to this story."

"I do understand what you're saying. The only trouble is you are putting yourself in considerable danger. I don't think you fully understand what's going on in this part of the world."

"That's the reason I'm here - so I can get to understand the situation - to learn. I've been well briefed. The biggest danger I will face may be from my own people, if that's the right phrase - armed Israelis. But I want to find out exactly what it's like to be on the other side of the fence - or in this case the barrier."

Janice fell silent again. She couldn't help but admire the recklessness and restlessness of youth. There was a time when she had been suffused with the same passion, the same sense of justice. She had become becalmed with age. She had grown to understand which side she was on and had become used to shutting her mind from the suffering and travails experienced on the other side. She was no longer the same young woman who had been stirred by the injustice of apartheid and who was constantly at odds with her friends and family. Her integration into Jewish Israeli society was now complete. And with that integration came an understanding that she didn't have to accept everything the Netanyahu government did was right, but when it came to the survival of her country and the future of her children she had to show her allegiance to her own kind.

Apart from occasional pleasantries when David was able to comment on the scenery and attractive surroundings of the district in which Janice lived, the rest of the journey was continued in silence.

The condominium was in a leafy part of Ramat Hasharon. There were signs of affluence, underscored by the upmarket properties and vehicles which marked out the territory. Janice's home was essentially in a 'gated community' and the vehicle was greeted by an armed security man at the entrance, where a barrier prevented them from driving straight in.

The security man waved them through with a smile and Janice steered the vehicle into an open courtyard area, surrounded by apartments on all four sides. They were all pristinely whitewashed with a preponderance of glass windows and patio doors ensuring the occupants were able to look out onto a swimming pool surrounded by a lawn expanse with a ring of palm trees providing a modicum of privacy. Each apartment had its own garage and Janice's obligingly opened its door as she drove towards it, pulling up just before the entrance.

"You might be better off getting out first David. These are quite narrow."

David climbed out and waited for his aunt to park the car. Once it was safely ensconced in the garage, Janice opened the boot and David removed his large backpack and a couple of carrier bags containing gifts for the Barlev family. David followed his aunt to the front door of her apartment which opened into a bright hallway. This led to a large living room which was appointed with expensive contemporary furniture including a large centrally positioned coffee table made from walnut. The table was the focal point for two large, oatmeal coloured sumptuous sofas on top of which were a cluster of carefully arranged brightly coloured cushions. Other matching walnut pieces were an entertainment unit, housing a large screen television, and a nest of side tables. The room was brightly lit by the morning sun through large patio doors which opened onto a seating area.

"Let me show you your room David," said Janice leading the way to a passage from which a range of doors led both right and left. The first door opened into a bedroom with a large double bed adorned with a blue and white patterned duvet and matching curtains.

"This is Ari's room. You haven't met him yet and he doesn't live here at the moment. He was called up last month, so won't be back for a while. Make yourself at home. There's a fair amount of cupboard space although it doesn't look as though you will need much."

"I always travel light," said David, dropping his backpack onto the floor.

Let me show you the rest of our home. It's quite small but suits us fine. Of course, you've seen Tziporah lately."

"Yes I actually saw her last weekend in Sheffield. I managed to pick her brain regarding my visit. She seems to be enjoying her course."

"Well this is her room," said Janice. "I can't remember the last time she used it though. I'm not sure she'll come back to live in Israel. What do you think?"

"She seems quite settled in England really. She's got a circle of good friends. I suppose it depends on what she can do with her degree eventually. I don't know whether the UK is crying out for pharmacists."

"Ah well I can't complain. I did the same to my parents. I'm sure you know Ari is based in Jerusalem. Assuming he can get some leave, I hope you will be able to see him before you leave."

"I will do my best Aunty Janice. I must get his number from you before I leave for Jerusalem."

The brief tour of the apartment continued. When it was over, David took a shower and joined his aunt on the small patio overlooking the pool in the square. She was flat on her back soaking up the late morning sunshine. Two lads were throwing a ball to each other, their voices echoing around the square. David had a smattering of Hebrew but not enough to follow their exuberant shouting. Prior to his barmitzvah his parents had ensured he attended lessons held in the local synagogue in south Hampstead. That was as far as it went. On reaching the so-called status of Jewish male adulthood the visits to the 'cheder' ended and he was free to enjoy a normal adolescence along with his many school friends.

Once he began life at university in Sussex David began to look outwards, eschewing much of his Jewish heritage. He became involved in student politics, eventually joining a local Young Socialist group where he began to develop an antagonism to Zionism. This led to membership of Jews for a Free Palestine where he honed his views and began to become active in support of the Palestinian cause. His parents began to view his political activities with alarm and were particularly affronted when he spoke of his Jewish upbringing as the "monkey on my back."

After a few minutes, the exuberance of the two youths subsided. They had climbed out of the pool and were now walking back to their apartment on the opposite side of the square. David watched them disappear through the front door.

"So what are your feelings about arriving in the Jewish homeland?" asked his aunt, exploiting the sudden silence. "Does any of this strike a chord?"

"There's no doubt it does," said David. "It's obviously a special country for Jews. But I keep reminding myself that if I were a Palestinian it would *also* mean something special to me."

"The problem is co-existence is out of the question. Too much has happened in the past seventy years or so for there to be any trust between our two peoples."

"An even bigger problem is the thought of further decades of conflict and leaving in fortress conditions. Surely concessions need to be made on both sides."

Janice sat up straight and turned to her nephew. "It's much easier to say that from the outside. For those of us living in Israel 'concession' is not such a simple concept. The idea of losing our country and its status as the *Jewish* homeland cannot be contemplated. There is too much at stake for us Israelis. We are the only true democracy in this part of the world. Whatever the world thinks about Netanyahu and our government, at least we can kick them out at the next election. Syrians can't get rid of Assad. The so-called Arab Spring has not produced democracy in those countries. Israelis can use any platform to condemn their government without fearing a prison sentence or worse."

David marvelled at his aunt's passionate response. She was certainly a force to be reckoned with when in full flow.

"My dad tells stories about you when you were my age."

Janice smiled. "Really? What sort of stories does he tell?"

"I'm told you were a bit of a rebel. You were politically active and apparently could've got into a lot of trouble."

"I think that's a bit of an exaggeration. I was more vocal than involved. I had a boyfriend who got into a lot of trouble. Actually, he landed up in prison for his efforts, ultimately with disastrous consequences.

"You must be pleased with the way things have worked out in South Arica," said David.

"Yes I am. It happened in spite of me rather than because of me. I abandoned the country of my birth a long time ago. Mind you, there are some serious problems ahead - it hasn't been plain sailing."

"What you said earlier, about .. you know.. 'coexistence' ... don't you think that could apply to South Africa?"

"I'm not sure what you mean," said Janice.

"Well after all that happened would you say there is trust between the different population groups?"

"Up to a point," said Janice. "The level of crime, some of it inter-racial, is still worrying by any standard. Apartheid may be officially over but the country still faces a long road ahead-"

"To where?" interjected David.

"Normality? If there is such a thing as a normal society."

"Well it's a democracy. Certainly, more democratic than during the apartheid years. Of course, I don't remember much. I was ten when we left. It's not unusual to hear South African accents in London these days. Many whites have left in recent years. They've found it difficult to embrace the new, democratic, integrated South Africa."

"Would you like to go back as a visitor?" asked Janice. "Perhaps you need to go on a 'fact-finding mission' to the land of your birth as well."

"One day ... yes one day I will go and find out for myself."

"As you are here for so short a time, would you like to visit your grandfather this afternoon?" asked Janice.

"Are you going anyway? I did promise my dad I would."

"I was going to go, depending on your plans," said Janice. "I'm sure he would love to see you. "

"How's he doing? Is he happy in the home?"

"He's doing fine. He's made a few friends. He's not very mobile but manages to get around with a walking frame. When did you last see him?"

"I guess when he visited us in England about seven years ago."

"You'll see a big change. He's very frail but fortunately he still has his mental faculties."

***

Martin Levy sat in his armchair gazing out of the window of his ground floor room which opened out onto a small, neatly maintained garden. It was well populated with a variety of shrubs with a bird table prominently positioned in the far corner. A warbler of some sort, having fed from the table, had disappeared into a large yellow shrub and Martin was awaiting its emergence so he could identify it more accurately.

Having lived in a small one-bedroom apartment for several years following his emigration from South Africa, Martin had reluctantly agreed to make the move to a care home where his increasing physical needs might be catered for on a more regular and effective basis. His rheumatoid arthritis had taken hold, rendering him unable to move around with any confidence. Having had several falls and a couple of serious cooking incidents when he had burnt his hands, it was suggested he be moved to a residential home in the Tel Aviv area, as close as possible to Janice. After much discussion and persuasion Martin had eventually agreed to the move to Neveh Shalom where he had lived comfortably and contentedly for the past four years.

"Hello Grandpa! How are you?" David approached and kissed Martin on the forehead.

"David! My boy! How wonderful to see you! Janice told me you were coming."

"Hello Dad," said Janice kissing her father and helping him to lean forward slightly as she rearranged the pillow behind his back.

"So when did this young man arrive?"

"This morning," said David. "I couldn't wait to see you."

"Thank you for coming," said Martin. "How's your dad? And your brother? And of course, your mother - how is she?"

"Everyone's well thanks Grandpa. They all send their love. So, this is nice. Very pleasant surroundings. Are you happy here?"

"Very. They do a good job of looking after everyone. I'm very lucky. It can be lonely sometimes, but then of course I get visitors. Jan takes me out from time to time, don't you darling."

"I do. Grandpa loves to drive along the beach front at Haifa. Shall we show David around? Fancy a walk?"

"That *would* be good," said Martin.

Janice bent down and hooked her arms under Martin's armpits while he slowly rose to his feet. "Can you pass us the zimmer please David? It's next to that cupboard."

Neveh Shalom was a modern residential home with about 50 residents, each with their own one-bedroom apartment. The apartments were furnished with en suite facilities.

Martin, Janice and David made their way along the long corridor at the end of which was a large, brightly-lit lounge area where some of the residents were playing chess, reading or watching the large screen television which occupied a far corner.

"This is where it all happens," said Martin. "Concerts, films, bingo and other communal events. There's a shabbas service in here every Friday evening."

They continued the tour through the lounge which led into a large dining room. There was a mixture of small square tables designed to seat one or two diners and larger round tables which would comfortably seat up to six people. Along one wall were several large windows providing a view of the garden. The windows were flanked by a set of enormous French doors leading to a patio area with further tables and chairs for al fresco dining. The walls were adorned with prints of paintings done by local artists, most of which depicted the surrounding area.

David and Janice followed Martin out into the garden where he sat down on a wooden bench.

"Why don't I leave you two men while I do some shopping? You've got lots of catching up to do. There's a supermarket about a kilometre away. I'll be about half an hour at the most."

"That's fine darling," said Martin.

"Good idea," said David. "See you later." David sat on the bench beside Martin as Janice left them.

"This is not bad at all," said David. "Do you sit out here often?"

"I do," said Martin." I love listening to the birds and watching them come to the feeder. So, young man what are you going to be up to while you are in Israel?"

David was taken aback by the sudden change of tack in his grandfathers' question. "What am I up to? I'm here to find out more about the political situation and in particular the Palestinian question."

"Does your father know about your plans?"

"He does. We had a long chat about my itinerary before I left."

"And what did he have to say?" Martin placed his hand firmly on David's arm.

"He wasn't exactly thrilled," said David, standing up. He went over to the bird table gathering his thoughts as he walked. He wanted to avoid any acrimony and was determined to avoid any further discussion if possible.

"I hope you know what you are doing," said Martin.

"I do. I just want to find out what's going on in this country. I've mostly had one side of the story and I need to gain a more balanced view of things."

"So how do you plan to find out more?" asked Martin.

David returned to the bench where he sat down next to his grandfather, placing an arm around his shoulders. "I've got some contacts in the West Bank who will look after me and make sure I'm fully briefed. I've got a completely open mind."

"How open are *their* minds? More to the point."

"I'll soon find out," said David. "I've also got meetings arranged with Jewish Israelis. Soldiers currently serving in the army as it happens. And just to make sure you know the full story I'll be spending a couple of days with a family in Gaza."

Martin didn't offer a response. After a few minutes he made an attempt to stand. David held on to his walking frame while he steadied himself. The walk back to Martin's flat was made in silence. Nothing was said until Martin was back in his armchair.

"Shall we have some tea?" asked Martin. "Inside that cupboard is a kitchenette."

"I'll make us a cuppa. Have you got any biscuits?"

"I can do better than that. Your aunt brought me a cake a couple of days ago. There's still plenty left. There's a tin in the cupboard below."

David made two cups of tea and cut a slice each of Janice's cake. He pulled up a chair and sat opposite Martin.

"So Grandpa, do you miss South Africa.?"

"I suppose I do. I was born and brought up there and spent seventy years of my life there."

"What about life here? Are you settled?"

"When you get to my stage of life your opportunities for living a full and active life are very limited. I don't think it would matter too much where I was right now. My world is this room, this home."

"How is your Hebrew?"

"Not wonderful. I understand more than I can speak. I do get by if I have to. Luckily there's a lot of English spoken here. There are immigrants from all over, so English is the common language for a lot of people."

On the wall above the television set in Martin's lounge area was a painting of Table Mountain. David went over to examine it. The artist was Stephen Jacobs.

"Do you know him? Stephen Jacobs?"

"Yes, his father was a very good friend of mine. Barney Jacobs. Stephen now lives in London. As you can see he's a talented artist."

"What do you miss most about South Africa? It must have changed a lot since the ANC got in. I don't remember too much. I was quite young when we left."

"I miss the life I had there - but I was younger then. I would probably have ended up in a home like this had I stayed. But then there's my friends of course."

"So are you South African, Israeli or what? Maybe you're both."

"No I think I'm still South African. I'm still not used to the Israeli ways of doing things."

"What makes you South African? I wonder what it is that makes a person claim their nationality. What exactly makes anyone a South African?"

"I suppose it's the many cultural aspects of life in that country. The way of life, the language or should I say the many languages, the food, the music, the sport-"

"But Grandpa what makes *you* a South African might be very different for a black person of your age in South Africa. My dad has a British passport and seems to identify himself with the British way of life. And yet when it comes to watching South Africa play England at rugby or cricket I hear him shouting for South Africa. I find that strange."

"You can't always rationalise these things. Often it's what you feel rather than what you think."

"Aunty Jan of course had a completely different view of South Africa back in the seventies when, according to my dad, she was a bit of a rebel. What she wanted for her country was completely different from what my dad or you wanted. Is that right?'

"It's right David. She was always uncomfortable about our attitudes and the lifestyle we had. I think she was more than happy to look for a new life over here and turn her back on her South African heritage."

"I didn't turn my back on it!" Janice had walked in to hear that she was the subject of the conversation.

"I was just hearing about what a rebel you were when you were younger. Maybe I'm following in your footsteps."

"I might have been a bit of a rebel but I certainly didn't deliberately turn my back on the country of my birth. I came over here like most of my friends as we looked to Israel as our Jewish homeland. I just happened to find it easy to settle here. Instead of turning my back on the country of my birth I fell in love with *this* country. In the end, it had less to do with my Jewishness than I realised. Anyway, we need to make a move David. Is that okay Dad? It's already late afternoon and Yossi will be home soon."

Martin stretched out a hand to his grandson. David stood up and took his hand.

"Thank you for coming David," said Martin. "Just be careful. That's all I ask - all I *can* ask."

"David bent down to kiss his grandfather. "I will. I promise. I'll see you soon."

***

Yossi Barlev returned to his apartment early that evening. He and David exchanged pleasantries while Janice stayed in the kitchen, preparing the evening meal. Yossi went to have shower leaving his guest to watch the news on BBC World. The refugee crisis across Europe showed no signs of going away with Greece bearing the brunt of the thousands seeking a better life, having escaped from the war zones of Syria, Iraq and Afghanistan. The wreckage of Aleppo and its displaced citizens was almost a daily news item. The rebels who had gone into hiding continued to make life difficult for the Syrian forces with occasional sorties holding up the rebuilding programme.

It was clear that Yossi had been forewarned about his wife's nephew's research mission and he avoided any controversy in that regard. The sooner the young man was out of his way the better was his preference. He was not particularly pleased that his house guest was a potential friend of the 'enemy'. Even so he managed to keep his tongue in check for the rest of the evening and by the time David left for Jerusalem in the morning, Yossi had already left for work at the hospital.

***

The coach had dropped David at the central bus station in Jerusalem. He entered the building and looked for the information kiosk where he was to meet his contact from Jews for a Free Palestine. David removed his large rucksack. His shirt was wet through with perspiration. The journey from Tel Aviv had been made in a bus with no air-conditioning. The window above David's seat was stuck and after several attempts at trying to open it he eventually gave up and drew on his reserves of patience in order to see out the rest of the journey.

Other passengers appeared used to the experience and were able to have noisy conversations. In particular, throughout the journey a couple behind David were engaged in a rather animated and often heated discussion, much of which was of little entertainment or interest value owing to his limited knowledge and experience of spoken Hebrew.

"David Levy?" The voice had the familiar timbre which characterised the South African accent of his grandfather. David turned round to see a young woman whose unkempt light brown shoulder-length hair and carelessly thrown together attire belied her exceptional good looks. She had the air of someone who had little time to spend in front of a mirror. Her deep blue eyes had a look of urgency which impressed on David the need to hurry.

"Hello you must be Rivkah!" David extended his hand which was received by a firm grip which took him by surprise.

"Sorry I'm a bit late," said Rivkah. "Come with me, my friend is waiting for us outside."

The walk took about five minutes. Rivkah led the way at a pace which David found difficult to maintain. She weaved in and out of human traffic at bewildering speed and David panicked for a couple of moments fearing he might lose her.

Eventually Rivkah stopped beside a blue Opel Corsa which was parked in a side street in a line of other vehicles. The driver, a tall, sturdily built young man with jet back hair and pale brown skin leapt out of the car and opened the boot which was chaotically filled with an assortment of bags, newspapers and boxes. There was barely enough room for David's bag which caused the parcel shelf to lift out of place once the boot was closed.

"Meet Yigal," said Rivkah.

"Shalom David!" Yigal proffered a large hand with exceptionally rough skin, engulfing David's, while his left hand opened the rear passenger side door. David climbed in the back, immediately noticing the overpowering smell of cigarette smoke. Indeed, before starting the engine Yigal lit up two cigarettes giving one to Rivkah who settled into the front passenger seat. He offered one to David who declined and immediately opened his window a few inches.

"We will drive thirty minutes," said Yigal pulling out of the parking space and joining the slow-moving traffic on the road out of the city centre.

"Where are we going?' asked David, making eye contact with the driver in his rear-view mirror.

"You are going Ramallah. Before we enter Ramallah we meet your contact. From Ramallah your contact look after you."

Rivkah turned round so she could see David. "Everything is organised for you. We have arranged your permit and there should be no problem entering Ramallah."

The traffic moved slowly for a while and suddenly they were on an open road and Yigal was able to increase their speed. The wind on David's face made a pleasant change and to some extent dissipated the offensive cigarette smoke.

"How long have you lived here, Rivkah" asked David after a few moments. "Your Hebrew is very fluent."

"I left South Africa when I was twenty, so in total about five years now."

"Have you still got family out there?"

"Yes my mother and stepfather are still there. I don't think they will ever leave."

"So, what made you come over here?"

Rivkah drew deeply on her cigarette and emitted a twin stream of smoke from her nostrils. David opened his window another couple of inches as surreptitiously as he could without causing offence.

"I wanted to see things for myself in this country and as I already had a cousin living here I decided to contact her and come on holiday. That was at the beginning of 2012. I suppose the holiday never really ended as I've stayed ever since. It just worked out that I became involved in JFP and it's become part of my life."

"Do you miss South Africa?"

"Not really. I was always restless living over there. Things had begun to take a turn for the worse anyway. The gloss of the Mandela years had begun to disappear and things were already turning sour. This has been quite a journey."

"Frying pan to the fire?"

"You could say that. This is such a volatile country. The hatred and resentment that is building up is just like the old South Africa - the one my parents grew up in."

After a half an hour or so of silence interrupted only by Yigal cursing the occasional errant driver, the infamous barrier came into view in the distance.

"That's the wall," declared Rivkah. "A terrible symbol for everyone who wants peace."

"It's chilling," said David. "Who would have thought something like that could exist in 2017."

"In the distance is the checkpoint," said Rivkah. "We have to drive through Qalandia first and then afterwards your contact will take you to Ramallah."

"Will that be a problem?" asked David straining to see the checkpoint in the distance. It looked more like a border crossing in size than the sort of checkpoint he had read about and seen pictured in print and on the internet.

"No, no problem," said Rivkah.

As they approached the checkpoint, queues of people could be seen waiting on both sides of the main gate. The queue on the opposite side was much longer and David could not see its end. The wall which had concrete panels slotted together had been daubed here and there with a range of graffiti, including some political slogans in English.

"I need your passport David," said Rivkah opening the car door.

"Sure. Must I come with you?"

"No you wait here. My friend is at the gate. I'll speak to him." Rivkah made her way over to the gate where the people were queueing. The gate was manned by soldiers carrying assault rifles. The soldiers were orchestrating the flow of pedestrians crossing into and out of Israeli territory. The pedestrians were funnelled slowly through caged tunnels.

After a few minutes Rivkah returned to the car. "Okay let's go," she said.

Yigal steered the car towards the line of vehicles entering at a separate checkpoint. When they reached the young soldier checking the details of occupants, Rivkah said something in Hebrew and they were waved through to the other side where they were on the outskirts of what appeared to be a town comprising a conglomeration of concrete buildings. The rooftops were adorned with large water tanks.

"What is this?' asked David. "Where are we now?"

"Qalandia Refugee Camp," said Rivkah.

"So *this* is Qalandia," said David. "Qalandia Camp? I was expecting a settlement of tents or shacks."

"It's more like a town," said Rivkah. "It's evolved over the years. The checkpoint and wall have been constructed to separate the village of Qalandia from the refugee camp. The village is about a kilometere and a half from here."

The 'camp' comprised a landscape of sprawling concrete boxes of assorted sizes. Some of the buildings appeared to be in an unfinished state awaiting window panes. Water tanks were perched on top of most of the houses.

"How long has the camp been here?" asked David.

"Virtually since the State of Israel was born," said Rivkah. "Some of the people living here have known nothing else. The UN set up a number of refugee camps to provide temporary homes for nearly three quarters of a million Palestinians who lost their homes in the late 1940s."

"And they've been here since?"

"That's right. The word 'temporary' is a bit of a joke. We are meeting our contact here. If you want to walk around Qalandia he will be happy to escort you."

"That would be good," said David, fumbling in his rucksack for his camera.

Yigal slowed the vehicle down and pulled over into a lay-by where another older more battered vehicle awaited their arrival. He climbed out at the same time as the driver of the other vehicle and they met each other half way. The two men embraced and Yigal gestured to David to join them.

"David, this is your contact Abed."

David shook hands with the man. "Pleased to meet you Abed."

The smile on Abed's face belied the narrative of his dark brown eyes which suggested a deep seated mixture of anger and resentment.

"I am pleased you come to visit us," said Abed, transmitting a genuine warmth.

"We leave you with Abed," said Yigal. "Abed is your guide."

"I will look after you," said Abed. "My English is not bad."

"Not bad?" said David. "Your English is very good. I'm very grateful to you."

Rivkah got out the car and went over to the three men. "How long do you want to stay in the West Bank, David?"

"Maybe a couple of days. What suits you. When will it be convenient to fetch me?"

Rivkah and Yigal exchanged a brief conversation in Hebrew.

"Yigal can fetch you on Wednesday or Thursday," said Rivkah. "So today is Monday. That will give you at least two days. You can phone us to confirm."

"That's great. Thanks a lot."

David was excluded from the conversation as the other three went over the arrangements in Hebrew. David took a photograph of them with the 'camp' in the distance. The dusty road was sprinkled with gravel and a passing car sent a small stone flying into David's shin. He nearly choked from the dust which filled the air immediately.

The tour of Qalandia camp lasted about an hour with several stops where David was encouraged to leave the car and explore. There were parts which resembled a war zone. Rubble heaped upon rubble. Walls pocked with bullet holes. Walls covered with Arabic graffiti and paintings of local heroes.

Qalandia Camp had grown since it was set up as a refuge for displaced Palestinians from villages throughout northern and central Palestine. Originally it was intended to provide temporary accommodation for some five thousand refugees. But as it became clear that its temporary status was unlikely to be resolved, the population swelled to its current unofficial figure of nearly twelve thousand.

Abed's Fiat Punto had a front passenger seat which was barely fixed to the floor of the vehicle. Abed pulled away from his parking spot and then stopped suddenly as a goat stepped in front. David was thrown forward almost meeting the dashboard with his chin. The seatbelt was not functional, having lost its buckle, so David was obliged to grip the door handle tightly for the rest of the journey to Ramallah. A loud knocking came from the rear of the car, a noise which did not seem to bother Abed in the slightest. Unfortunately for David, Abed was another chain smoker and had the passenger window winder been fully operational he would have been able to keep the window open throughout the journey to Ramallah. However, at a point about half an inch from the top, the window became stuck, allowing only a relatively small amount of fug to escape.

The journey to the destination in Ramallah took another thirty minutes or so.

***

"This is my sister, Aminah," said Abed. A young woman stood in the doorway, a welcoming smile lighting up her face which was framed by a cerise keffiyah. Her dark, sparkling eyes complemented the smile as she thrust out her hand to David.

"Welcome to Ramallah!"

"Thank you. I'm very pleased to be here," said David, taking her hand warmly.

Aminah beckoned to David to enter the gloomy hallway which led to a dimly-lit, somewhat cluttered lounge. A large table against the far wall was covered in piles of papers and books amongst which was a computer screen, keyboard and printer. The rest of the room had an assortment of seating including a large sofa, three non-matching chairs and some low stools. David imagined the many smoke-filled meetings which had taken place in this room.

"Would you like to try some Ramallah beer?" asked Abed, from the hallway.

"Yes please that would be good."

"Let me show you where you will be sleeping, "said Aminah. She led the way into a passage, which in turn led to a small room with a low camp bed and a canvas wardrobe with very little floor space left over. Owing to the shortage of windows, none of the rooms had seen much sunlight and the initial gloom seemed to pervade the entire house.

"I hope this will be okay," said Aminah. "You can put your rucksack on the bed for now."

"Very much okay," said David.

They returned to the living room where David ensconced himself in an armchair opposite Aminah. He sank low into the cushion which offered minimal resistance to his weight.

"So David, when did you arrive? What's your opinion of this country so far?

"I've only been in Israel for two days. I spent the first day with my aunt in Tel Aviv and came straight to the West Bank this morning. It's a bit early to form an opinion."

"We will take you into the city centre this evening if you want," said Aminah. "The night life here is excellent."

The English spoken by most of the people he had met so far had clearly been influenced by Americans. Presumably they had been taught by Americans or possibly picked up the accent from television programmes. However in Aminah's case David detected a different influence.

Thank you," said David. "Your English is very good, almost accent free. Have you spent some time in the UK?"

"I was at university in Sussex," said Aminah. I spent three years living in Brighton while I was studying for a politics degree. Abed has never been to England but he does okay with his English."

On cue, Abed entered with a glass of dark beer for David. "Here - you try this."

"Thank you Abed. It looks a good colour." David took a sip and nodded his approval. Aminah disappeared into the kitchen and returned a with a glass of sparkling water. She sat down opposite him, her dark eyes fixing on his. Her keffiyeh framed a face unmolested by make-up, yet impressively smooth and symmetrized with full, almost black eyebrows, a thin, straight nose and disproportionately small mouth. David thought her very beautiful as he studied the only features left exposed to the outside world. She wore a long crimson dress, embroidered with regular patterns of black with yellow zig-zag stitching. David's focus was drawn to a small rectangular area of exposed flesh at her neck.

"Tell me about your time in Brighton," said David.

"I loved Brighton. I loved my time at Sussex University." There was genuine enthusiasm in her response.

"Were you tempted to stay in England?"

"Of course it was tempting, but this is my home and I have my family to consider. My mother is an elderly widow and she can't just be left to fend for herself."

"Does she live here? With you?"

"She lives next door. Between Abed and me we keep an eye on her. We can make sure she is alright. What about you David? A young Jewish man in the West Bank?"

"I'm here to learn," said David. "It goes without saying that we Jews get a distorted picture of Palestine. Israel can do no wrong."

"I've never understood the psyche of Jews in the Diaspora," said Aminah. "Their concept of nationalism. I mean what is their primary allegiance? I knew many Jews at Sussex who looked to Israel as their spiritual homeland but who had no intention of ever coming here to settle. They retained their British citizenship yet their nationalist schizophrenia meant they still embraced the Israeli cause."

Aminah's impeccable English had the precision of someone who had learned the language in its purest form. David had always marvelled at the lack of idiom in the English spoken by many foreigners. Yet living in Brighton for an extended period had 'tainted' Aminah's English with occasional expressions such as 'keep an eye on her.'

"I think that's a common problem with Jews in the diaspora," said David. "Living in South Africa, my parents had a more complicated form of that condition, what *you* call 'nationalist schizophrenia'. They always had the intention of leaving the country of their birth but were determined to settle in the UK and not Israel."

"But were they Zionists?"

"In the same way that most Jews are automatically Zionists. I think what complicated things more was the fact that their Zionism had a religious basis but neither of them was particularly religious."

"Don't all Jews predicate their Zionism on the text of the Old Testament?" Aminah took a cigarette from the pack on the table beside her chair. She offered one to David who declined. "Sorry it's a habit I developed at university. I only have about five a day. It keeps me sane."

"Don't mind me," said David. "Fortunately I never started - probably never will."

Aminah lit her cigarette and continued. "Without reference to the Land of Israel in the Bible surely Zionism would have no basis at all. The fact that Uganda was rejected as an alternative to Israel proves that point. What I can't grasp is the fact that so many Zionists are not religious."

"Then of course you have the Neturei Karta."

"Yes the supreme irony. The more you try to rationalise Zionism the more entangled your argument becomes."

David finished the last drop of beer.

"Some would argue that there is a de facto basis to the Jews' claim to Israel. There have been Jews here throughout the ages."

"I would never deny their claim to a stake in this land," said Aminah. "However there are more Jews outside than inside Israel and you have to ask why that is the case."

"There are many Jews, particularly in the UK, who support the Palestinian cause. I forgot to say that Sam Lurie sends his best wishes. He's the chair-"

"I know Sam, well. Yes, I know he's the chair of the JFP. He and I were at university together at Sussex. That's where we met."

"Sam and I go back a long way. He persuaded me to join the JFP a couple of years ago."

"How are you regarded by other Jews in your society? I mean being a member of the JFP must be difficult for a young Jewish man in North London."

"I'm not the most popular Jew in town," said David. "I've brought shame and embarrassment on my parents of course."

"Do you attend synagogue?"

"The last time I did was when I attended a family wedding."

"So you were born in South Africa. You went to live in Britain. What does that make you? Do you identify with South Africa at all?"

"Sort of. I suppose I am really British .... now. I'm not sure what that means. Am I also English? I live in England. Have I got anything in common with someone from Northern Ireland? The Outer Hebrides?"

"And your aunt? Is she an immigrant? Or is she a sabra?"

"My aunt is an interesting case. Definitely not a sabra. She was politically active in South Africa in the 70s and then came over to Israel as most young Jews did in those days. Not to settle - just for a taste of the 'homeland'."

Aminah smiled wryly. She stubbed out her cigarette. "So she decided to stay?" Her dark eyes were firmly fixed on his. David suddenly felt uncomfortable and shifted slightly in his seat.

"Yes she decided to stay."

"Of course that was her right."

"Yes as it is the right of all Jews."

The eyes didn't blink and remained fixed on his. "Don't you find that a bit strange? Maybe *strange* is not the appropriate word...." Aminah appeared to search for an alternative.

David leant back and crossed his legs, using the change of position to avert his eyes momentarily. He had always been so sure of himself in discussions and debates in his role as member of the JFP. Now confronted with the reality of a Palestinian armed with a sense of injustice, his own role as a supporter of her cause was diminishing by the second. It was impossible to avoid patronisation and he was not sure how to deal with this increasing sense of inadequacy. Reducing the conversation to a more specific, more personal level had diminished his ability to argue in the sort of generalities he was used to when putting the Palestinian case on the campus or at public meetings back in England. Moreover, the focus on his family had introduced an unsettling feeling of guilt.

Aminah was immediately sensitive to his discomfort. She smiled and the sparkle returned to her eyes. "David we appreciate what you and the JFP are doing. It must be difficult to go against your own people."

"I can't avoid feeling a little guilty - responsible in some way."

Aminah leant forward and smiled. "There's no need to take on the guilt of others. I respect and appreciate your concern and if only we could get through to other Jews - other Jews both inside and outside Israel."

"Do you not think there's a barrier of mistrust between both sides?" said David shifting his position in the chair. I'm not sure all this talk of a two-state solution helps. What do you think?"

"What do I think? I think too much has happened over the past six or seven decades. I think that's probably an impossible barrier to break down at the moment. You need to consider all those generations of children who have grown up on both sides - I can only speak from the Palestinian side. Palestinian children only know Israelis as people in military uniform who bear arms. They have grown up thinking they should be targets of stone throwing. Yes, we have propaganda in our schools, in our homes, in our media. How do you break down barriers built up by such propaganda, let alone the personal experience of young people? It's impossible."

"What about the role of America? Isn't that a huge factor in all this?"

"Some of my friends and colleagues think that America is *the* problem," said Aminah sitting back again. She reached for her pack of cigarettes. David watched her flick her lighter and light the cigarette held loosely between her long fingers. David thought that she lit a cigarette with such elegance it almost made smoking appear a respectable and sophisticated activity. She inhaled and emitted a stream of smoke sideways careful to avoid directing any in David's direction. "Yes, if America adopted a more neutral stance that would be a good start."

"Of course the Jewish lobby is key when it comes to American policy in this region." declared David reverting to the more comfortable role as spokesperson for JFP.

"We are always presented as the villains who want to drive the Israelis into the Mediterranean. Israelis need to understand that we are ordinary people who want to be citizens of our own country. Anyway David we need to make sure you have a good time in Ramallah. Would you like to join me and Abed in one of our night clubs tonight? I can promise you a good time."

"Well it's either that or an early night," said David. "I need some action to wake me up."

***

"Your brother is Skyping you," said Yossi, taking the tablet to the kitchen where Janice was cutting vegetables. She wiped her hands on the apron and took the tablet, placing it on its stand on the kitchen unit. Jonathan's face filled the screen smiling at her somewhat inanely. Janice always found these occasions awkward as all too often the communicants would talk over each other. It had made her realise the importance of body language in conversations. Similarly, she had always found telephone conversations even more difficult.

"Shalom sister," said Jonathan. "How are things there? How's my son getting on? I hope he isn't driving you two mad!"

"No he isn't. Actually, he's not with us at the moment."

"How come?"

"He's taken himself off to the West Bank for a few days."

"He said he was going there on an official visit but I didn't know he was going for more than just a day."

"Honestly Jonnnie I'm not sure exactly how long he will be there. He said he would let us know when he was coming back to Tel Aviv."

"I'm secretly hoping he will get it out of his system. This JFP nonsense is driving us mad back home here in England. Maybe you can get to work on him. I'm sure Yossi won't tolerate his weird ideas."

"I think you will have to let him reach his own conclusions Jonnie. He's a bright boy and like most young people he needs to go through a period of radicalism. Mind you, come to think of it - you missed all that."

"There was only room for one firebrand in our family at that time. Can you imagine what it would have done to our parents had I gone all radical on them? No I was a model son playing it straight down the line."

"I wonder who was on the right side back then in the bad old 70s."

"Yes but who stayed to witness the change? Who was it that left the land of her birth, her parents, her family home-"

"Was there not even an ounce of shame living such a privileged existence? Guilt maybe?"

"My loyalty was always to my family. I didn't choose to grow up in that society. Anyway, I'm not sure we should be having this discussion now. Strange that my son has inherited his aunt's genes. Just as well you've calmed down and matured in your views."

"Hold on a moment." Janice interrupted the chat to put a dish in the oven. She welcomed the break in the conversation which had taken a most unhelpful course. "Anyway," she continued, "I told David to make contact with you once he was in the West Bank. Unfortunately, he couldn't give me details of his accommodation or his contacts there. I am waiting to hear from him myself."

"If and when you do, can you let me know please Jan."

"I will. Anyway, I'd better concentrate on this dinner I'm supposed to be cooking tonight. Let's catch up again soon. Love to Paula."

***

Ramallah at night was as vibrant as any European city David had ever encountered. There were the usual bars, pavement cafes, noisy traffic and bustling crowds. He marvelled at the resourcefulness of a city which had survived an attempt to be downgraded and doused by its Israeli masters, yet had managed to maintain a stoicism of character which helped to maintain the surprisingly positive spirit evident in the West Bank.

David was surprised to hear so much western music. The dance floor shook to the flickering rhythm of gyrating, writhing figures. He felt as though he was trapped inside a giant zoetrope. Aminah took his hand and their two bodies began to move to the music. She had dispensed with the kaffiyeh and was wearing denim jeans and a sleeveless dark top. Her hair had fallen over the front to her chest, swishing and flailing as her body twisted and gyrated with more skill and panache that David could muster. He was torn between being led and stopping to admire the way her body adapted to the music.

He decided to let himself go and, surprised by his own fluidity and flexibility, he was swept along by the pounding of the music which invaded his head. He seemed to have lost control of his movements. His body had taken on a life of its own with its new-found freedom. It gyrated, it whirled, it undulated, it shook. All in unison with the young woman opposite him. He lost all sense of where he was and why he was there. Suddenly it stopped. The DJ had decided it was time to change the tempo. Aminah took David's hand and drew him towards her. David adjusted his movement as best he could, once again prepared to be led by Aminah. Her hair had a distinctive smell somewhere between 'nutty' and 'garlicky'. Unusual but not unpleasant.

When the dance was over she continued to hold his hand and led him to their table, where Abed was seated with another young man. He could not help noticing they were holding hands under the table.

Aminah and David returned to the dance floor a short while later. "Is your brother-"

"Yes he is," said Aminah.

"I didn't realise. Must he keep it secret?"

"Yes he must. I'm the only one who knows. We are not as tolerant as the West in this country," said Aminah. "Or Israel for that matter."

"Has he got a partner? Is he in a relationship?"

Aminah appeared not to have heard. They joined a group which had formed a large circle for a traditional Palestinian Dabke dance, usually but not exclusively performed at weddings.

For the rest of the night David managed to engage with a range of Aminah's friends taking the opportunity to both dance and chat outside away from the noise. He was pleasantly surprised at the warmth of the reception he received.

***

David opened his eyes. The room was still dark. It was always dark, regardless of the time of day. He groped for his phone lying on the floor next to the bed. It was 7.30. There was a stirring next to him. He felt a knee press against his side. His phone had provided sufficient light to enable him to see Aminah's sleeping face. She looked so peaceful. Beautiful, he thought. Strands of hair had fallen across her cheek. David returned his phone to the floor again. He turned over to face her and lay still, listening to her breathing.

Sleeping together had been the most natural conclusion to their evening. No words had been required. Aminah had taken complete control of events. She had initiated their first kiss. It was she that led him to her room, to her bed where they now lay in sublime intimacy. To David there was something profoundly symbolic about what had taken place since his arrival in Ramallah. A consummative event of the utmost significance. Given their different backgrounds, their night together had acquired a resonance capable of a life-long effect for both these two young people.

Aminah stirred once more, this time placing an arm across David's chest. "Good morning. What time is it?"

"It's nearly quarter to eight." David sat up and perched on the side of the bed, pulling on his trousers.

"Did you sleep okay, David?"

"Yes thanks. You?"

"Yes very well. I dreamt I was back in England; at Sussex University."

"Thank you for last night. I had a wonderful time," said David standing up to go to the bathroom.

"So did I. I'll organise some breakfast." Aminah got out of bed. Putting on her dressing gown she went through to the kitchen.

***

Breakfast was taken in silence, apart from occasional sounds of cutlery clinking on crockery. Both were deep in thought, reflecting on what had happened. David had already decided to move on from Ramallah that morning. He had planned to spend no more than a couple days in Ramallah anyway, but the turn of events had hastened his decision to leave for a different part of the West Bank. David was keen to take back control of his situation as soon as possible. Both he and Aminah had agreed it would be for the best. He would try to take a bus to Bethlehem, where Aminah would arrange for a friend to meet him.

"Where is Abed? I want to say goodbye to him," said David.

"I don't know,. He's not in the house," said Aminah.

"I'm going to pack and get ready to go. I hope he appears soon." David stood up and kissed Aminah on the forehead. "Thank you for everything. I'm very grateful to have met you."

Aminah smiled and squeezed his hand. This brief interlude in her life had been fortifying and rewarding. It was her first and only experience of intimacy with a Jew and it marked a significant, albeit extremely brief, milestone for her.

Just then the sound of shouting could be heard coming from the street outside. He and Aminah went to investigate. A large crowd of young people, mainly men, had gathered in a line across the street. Most were masked with keffiyehs. The first stone struck a parked car to the left about ten metres from David. It bounced harmlessly off the bonnet and pinged against a drainpipe, hanging loosely from the front wall of a neighbouring house. Suddenly a phalanx of soldiers appeared from a narrow alley fanning out into the street. Each soldier had a large plastic shield as he advanced towards the crowd at the opposite end.

David and Aminah hid behind the car and waited. A lump of concrete the size of a rugby ball hit one of the shields. Another lump of concrete followed, accompanied by a hail of stones which made a rattling sound as they made contact with the advancing shields.

The soldiers halted. Then a loud cry was followed by a single gun shot. A man at the front of the crowd slumped to the ground. Two men on either side dropped to their knees to attend to him while others scattered in different directions.

The crowd had thinned to a defiant dozen or so. Some were still chanting and gesticulating at the soldiers opposite. David hesitated, not sure whether to become involved. He looked at Aminah. "I have to help him!"

Aminah grasped his arm. "No don't. These people have no mercy."

David gently removed her arm. "I have to. I have no choice - a man is badly wounded."

Crouching low, David rushed across to help. There was a grimace of pain on the victim's face as he lay still on the rough road surface. A pool of blood had formed from the wound in his stomach despite the attempts to staunch the flow.

"I'm a medical student," said David, dropping to his knees. "Is he conscious?"

The two men attending to their wounded comrade didn't respond. They ignored him, apparently not understanding. David pointed to himself shouting

"Doctor!" At this, the men gave way allowing David to attend to their comrade. He bent over the fallen man whose eyes were closed. He had been shot in the stomach and had lost a lot of blood. He listened for breathing but the shouting was so loud it was impossible to hear. He felt for a pulse but there was nothing. David immediately tried mouth-to-mouth resuscitation but to no avail. Linking his fingers, he placed both hands on the man's chest and began to pump rhythmically. Again to no avail.

When David stood up shaking his head, those in the crowd who had remained, fell silent, probably in shock at their loss of a comrade. Then one of them stepped forward and hurled a lump of concrete across the divide. It bounced once on the road, rolling briefly before coming to rest a metre or so in front of the line of soldiers.

Another shot was fired, this time into the air, followed by an indistinct barking through a loud hailer. This was a signal for those opposite to resume their stone throwing.

Then another shot was fired. This time not from the soldiers, but from somewhere behind the crowd. An Israeli soldier fell to the ground clutching his leg. A further command from an Israeli officer prompted renewed firing. David was thrown backwards by an explosion of burning pain in his chest. He tried to stay on his feet as he swayed one way and then another. His tried to raise his hand to his chest as his knees began to give way. His vision was corrupted by a kaleidoscope of faces and houses and then blackness as the side of his head met the ground with a crack. It was the moment he ceased to exist.

Glossary

Waar is hy? — Where is he?

Dompas — Slang for pass (Black people were required to carry a 'pass') Dompas literally means 'dumb pass'

Suka wena — Go away!

Hamba! Los hom! — Go! Leave him!

Shiksa — A gentile girl or woman (derogatory)

Haw nkosasana — Literally princess – used affectionately to address a young woman

Shebeen — Illicit bar in a township

Khaya — Literally a house, but here referring to an outhouse for black domestic servants

Word wakker! — Wake up!

Ngena — Come

Barmitzvah — A ceremony for Jewish boys on attaining religious adulthood at the age of 13.

Takkies	Shoes similar to plimsolls, usually with laces.
Madam	The 'madam' was a term used for a white domestic employer in apartheid South Africa. Domestic servants would usually address their employers as Madam or Master.
Cheder	A school or classes for young Jewish children where they learn Hebrew and Jewish customs and traditions
Kaddish	A prayer said by a male mourner at an Orthodox Jewish funeral
Sabra	An Israeli citizen born in Israel
Bantustans	A territory set aside for black people under the policy of 'Separate Development' (Apartheid) e.g. Transkei
BOSS	Bureau of/for State Security. BOSS agents were feared by activists as once they were arrested, they were liable to be imprisoned without trial or detained for up to 180 days.

Printed in Great Britain
by Amazon